STEEL™

WARNER BROS. PRESENTS

A QUINCY JONES·DAVID SALZMAN ENTERTAINMENT PRODUCTION A KENNETH JOHNSON FILM SHAQUILLE O'NEAL "STEEL" ANNABETH GISH RICHARD ROUNDTREE and JUDD NELSON

MUSIC BY MERVYN WARREN PRODUCER MARK ALLAN EDITED BY JOHN F. LINK PRODUCTION DESIGNER GARY WISSNER DIRECTOR OF PHOTOGRAPHY MARK IRWIN, C.S.C./A.S.C. EXECUTIVE PRODUCERS SHAQUILLE O'NEAL LEONARD ARMATO BRUCE BINKOW

BASED UPON THE CHARACTERS PUBLISHED BY DC COMICS PRODUCED BY QUINCY JONES·DAVID SALZMAN & JOEL SIMON WRITTEN AND DIRECTED BY KENNETH JOHNSON

www.wbmovies.com/STEEL

STEEL™

A novel by

DEAN WESLEY SMITH

Based on the screenplay written by

KENNETH JOHNSON,

based upon characters published by
DC Comics

STEEL, created by

LOUISE SIMONSON
and JON BOGDANOVE

TOR®

A TOM DOHERTY ASSOCIATES BOOK
NEW YORK

This is a work of fiction. All the characters and events portrayed in this book are either products of the author's imagination or are used fictitiously.

STEEL

A Tor Book
Published by Tom Doherty Associates, Inc.
175 Fifth Avenue
New York, NY 10010

Tor Books on the World Wide Web:
http://www.tor.com

Tor® is a registered trademark of Tom Doherty Associates, Inc.

ISBN: 0-812-53931-1

First edition: July 1997

Printed in the United States of America

0 9 8 7 6 5 4 3 2 1

CHAPTER 1

THE THIN FOG HUGGED THE GROUND AMONG THE PINE trees, a white blanket over the sounds of the early morning. The sun had yet to break above the jagged mountains to the east, to slice through the sharp edge of coolness in the air. Every branch, every stone, still held the dampness of the night. Even the dirt that later in the day would be a dry, powdery dust, was now heavy and black with moisture.

No sound.

No movement.

Ten minutes before dawn. A magical time in the Arizona mountains.

John Henry Irons wished he could enjoy his surroundings, if for nothing more than a moment. He loved the mountains, especially a wilderness area like this one. But he didn't have a moment. He wasn't on vacation. He was here to work.

He lay stretched out on the rock and dirt of the forest floor, his huge seven-foot-two-inch frame hidden as best he could behind a row of scrub brush. Almost afraid to breathe, he remained totally unmoving. His full-body Army camouflage suit blended perfectly with the brush and dirt, and he hoped the ground fog would also help hide him.

In his large hands he held a brand-new invention he helped to create: the Heat-Pulse Antitank Rifle. HPAR for short. The weight of the gun felt almost reassuring to him, but his fingers were long past numb from the cold and damp.

A pointed rock jabbed into his upper thigh, but he ignored the slight pain. No movement. He desperately wanted to blow some hot air on his freezing fingers, but he didn't dare move or make a sound. Not now.

Ten paces to his right he knew Colonel Maxwell David hid, also in full camouflage. The colonel carried an Antitank Laser Cannon. A weapon strong enough to cut through solid steel. Or cut a human in half instantly.

Ten paces to the colonel's right was Sparks, the third member of their attack team. She also carried an AL Cannon. John Henry knew she wasn't as good a shot as the colonel. But she was no slouch, and if the colonel missed his target, she'd back him up instantly.

The fog around John Henry seemed to swirl slightly, as if restless.

Something was changing. He could sense it.

His grip tightened slightly on his weapon, but nothing else moved. It was as if he'd made his giant body part of the rocks, dirt, and brush.

The tank was coming.

He knew it almost before he felt the rumble through the ground under his stomach. His right finger moved slightly, clicking the HPAR into active status. A faint hum reassured him. He was now armed.

And very deadly.

Thunder slowly filled the air, shaking the pine needles, raining moisture down on the forest floor. Under him the ground was now shaking like a faint, constant earthquake.

Then, almost as if in slow motion, the tank came over the top of the rise a hundred paces in front of him. It seemed to pause—huge, thick turret pointed into the sky—before the front dropped down and the barrel of the gun swung onto a direct line to where he hid in the brush.

He held his breath, not even blinking. The key was to not be seen until the colonel fired. Otherwise the mission might be completely blown.

The rumble of the gigantic machine filled the forest around him. In all his years in the Army he'd never faced anything this big before. He'd stood beside many tanks and even crawled around inside one once. He knew how they worked, what electronics they carried, and the power of the big gun. He had done all the training and all the work, but now the moment of truth was at hand.

Could he stop one?

A blue laser beam cut at the tank from the colonel's position, burning off the top of a greenish-white bush in a slight puff of gray smoke.

White-hot flames flew as if a welding torch had cut into the tank's side. The heavy metal tread of the tank screamed the sounds of tearing metal as the tank spun sideways.

The tearing of metal shook the forest as the heavy tank tread ripped apart faster than the driver of the tank could get his huge machine stopped.

Perfect. The colonel had hit his mark. The tank wouldn't be moving again for some time.

Like the sound of a heavy metal door opening, the tank turret moved, turning back to aim at the colonel's location.

As the turret lowered to find its target, John Henry brought up the HPAR, aimed quickly at the center of the tank, and pulled the trigger.

With a familiar kick and a wash of heat back over his face, a pulse of ball lightning flashed at the tank.

Around the tank the air crackled and turned blue as electrical charges surrounded the tank. John Henry knew at that moment the tank's instruments were going crazy inside, shutting down one after the other.

An electromagnetic pulse overload.

John Henry fired again.

Another direct hit.

The tank seemed to light up with the pulsing energy surrounding it. John Henry knew that all the tank's electronics were now completely dead. And the electrical charges were starting to heat up the tank's metal.

He fired once more, another direct hit.

By now the exterior of the tank was clearly heating up, some outer points of metal turning slightly red as the blue electrical pulses formed a ball around the giant killing machine.

Suddenly the top hatch of the tank popped open and a soldier climbed quickly out.

"That's enough!" he shouted. "That's enough. My ass is on fire, for God's sake."

Another soldier climbed quickly from the front hatch while a third jumped from the top, both doing their best not to touch the tank they were climbing out of.

Three crew. Safe.

Good. All of them were out, moving away from the tank, hands in the air in the traditional sign of surrender. None of them had been hurt besides a few superficial burns.

John Henry exhaled and then relaxed.

Beside him Colonel Maxwell David climbed to his feet, laughing. At five ten, and fifty years of age, he was in the best physical shape possible. If he wasn't working in the department, he was working out in the gym. Now his barrel laughs echoed through the trees around them like distant gunshots.

"Thought I smelled some nuts roasting," he said, and again laughed. "Call it, Sparks."

Ten paces from the colonel, Sparks climbed to her feet and keyed her walkie. "This is Little John," she said. "We've shot the Sheriff."

"I'll say we did," the colonel said, laughing at the three tank crew members as they inspected their hands for burns.

"First weapons test terminated," Sparks continued to say into her talkie. "Back up all telemetry."

She snapped off her official communication and turned to where John Henry sat. "Nice shooting, Johnny."

"Thanks," John Henry said, smiling at her as he pushed his body off the ground and stood. His muscles were tight from the hard surface and the cold. He stretched and then ignored the pains. The success of the weapon in his hands was more than he had hoped for.

He pulled the gun up to his shoulder and aimed it at the dead tank. "You know, Sparky, moving the capacitors toward the stock really fixed the balance."

"Thanks," Sparks said, smiling at him. "Always glad to help out."

John Henry held her gaze for a moment, staring into her full blue eyes. He could see she was just as pleased at their success as he was. She was his best friend, all five feet two inches of her. And the best person with computers and numbers that he'd ever seen. The two of them made a great team.

From out of the brush behind and up the hill from

John Henry there was a crashing sound. Then Lieutenant
Nathaniel Burke appeared ahead of Senator Maggie Nolan. Burke wore a brown suit and polished brown shoes,
completely out of place in the forest. He carried a large
suitcase full of video equipment. His job had been to
record the test from up on the hill, far enough away to
be out of any possible danger.

John Henry glanced over at Sparks and shook his head
as Burke stumbled and almost fell over a small log. She
managed to not laugh, even though it was clear she
wanted to. They both didn't much care for Burke. He
was a squirrelly little guy who always wanted to be the
center of attention. John Henry put up with him, mostly
because he was so good at weapons development.

Senator Nolan from Colorado, at sixty, looked very
comfortable in her jeans and a ski parka, as if she'd been
wearing them most of her life. Her hands were stuffed
deep into her pockets and she seemed to be keeping her
distance behind Burke coming down the hill. John Henry
didn't blame her. He liked to keep his distance from
Burke, too.

"Wow!" Burke said, moving up beside the tank and
looking it over. Then he moved down to where Sparks
and John Henry stood. "Worked just as we planned."

"I'd say better," Sparks said. "Wouldn't you, Colonel?"

"Put it this way," the colonel said. "No tank is going
to want to run into this weapon."

"I'll drink to that," one of the tank crew said. "Just
make sure the other side doesn't get it."

John Henry laughed and relaxed a little more. He
didn't realize just how nervous he had become about
these days of testing.

"Come on, Senator," the colonel said. "Let's take a
closer look. Burke, get that video up here. I want close-

ups of the tank and the locations of the firing positions.''

''On it, sir,'' Burke said.

He picked up the suitcase as the colonel and the senator made their way through the brush toward the destroyed tank.

Burke turned to Sparks, ignoring John Henry. ''How do you always manage to make camo gear look like Victoria's Secret?''

Sparks laughed, then with a glance at John Henry, said, ''This *is* Victoria's Secret. You wouldn't want to *see* my camo.''

Burke smiled and in a low whisper to Sparks he said, ''I'd be willing to give you a shot.''

''Oh, lucky me.''

She nodded to John Henry and the two of them followed the senator and colonel toward the tank, leaving Burke alone.

Behind them Burke stared at Sparks, his face red, his anger boiling just below the surface. He didn't like rejection. He didn't like it one bit.

''Payback's a bitch,'' he said under his breath.

CHAPTER 2

THE COOLNESS OF THE EARLY MORNING STILL HADN'T left the forest around the ruined Army tank. The fog had lifted somewhat and now only slight wisps of white drifted among the pine trees. The sun brushed the tops of the trees and the mountains beyond with an orange and red sunrise, giving only a hint of the heat of the day to come.

John Henry Irons finished inspecting the damage to the tank, then listened to the description from the tank commander about the conditions inside the tank during the attack.

"Hot!" was the word he used the most. Just simply hot.

It was all exactly as John Henry had expected, and as the colonel had planned. The new weapon had worked. It was a complete success. He could feel the tension ease even more.

John Henry turned back to Sparks, the HPAR still in his hands.

"How's the voltage holding, Johnny?" Sparks asked, indicating the weapon he held.

He glanced at the gauge on the side of the stock. The arrow was clearly pegged in the green. "Solid. Still got fifty-seven megs. Not bad after three full shots."

Sparks nodded. "Not bad at all. You might have gotten another five at least from it. Let me check the amp curve."

John Henry held the gun out in front of her and kept it steady as she punched through the stats of the weapon's LED readout.

After only a moment she said, "Perfect. Did your new alloy keep the barrel cool?"

"Cool, just like you," John Henry said, pointing a long finger at her.

She smiled and pointed back, touching the tip of her small finger against the fat tip of his. The movement had been a ritual of theirs for years and right now, after such a successful test, it felt like a wonderful sign-off.

After finishing the site filming, Lieutenant Nathaniel Burke watched John Henry and Sparks go through their stupid touching-finger bit. Over the last year he'd seen them do the same damn thing a hundred times and he was getting tired of it. Someday the giant guy would be long gone and he'd have Sparks to himself.

Someday, he'd—

"Got all the film you need, Lieutenant Burke?"

Burke spun around to face the stern face of the senator. "Yes, ma'am. Just about ready to go."

"Good," she said, glancing back at the tank.

"Impressed, ma'am?"

She nodded. "It's amazing weaponry. No doubt about it. Well worth the expenditure, as far as I can tell."

Then she turned to face Burke. "Was this the weapon's maximum power?"

Burke tucked the camera into its case and snapped the

lid closed. "Well, Senator," he said, then paused. "Is that what they told you?"

Then before she could answer he asked, "Forgive me for asking, ma'am, but what's your security clearance?"

She smiled at him like she would smile at a page on the Senate floor. "Level four."

Burke nodded, obviously not seeing her look, or understanding it. He stepped up close to her. He whispered, "Then it's okay for me to let you know."

He glanced around to see if anyone was close by, then turned back to her. "I've personally made some adjustments that up the intensity. Both on this weapon and on some of the others the team has been working on."

"How much?" she asked. "Enough to melt that tank's skin, for instance?"

"Let's just say, *considerably*," he said, then looked up and smiled at her.

"That would be something to see," she said.

"Always just trying to give my personal best in the service of my country."

The senator laughed. "Well, Lieutenant Burke. Keep it up and, who knows, you might even make captain in no time at all."

"Yes, ma'am," he said.

Behind them the colonel said, "Senator Nolan, if you're ready, I'll walk you back to the transport. Next stop on the fireworks tour: Tucson."

"On my way, Colonel," she said. Then with a final, private glance at Burke, she moved off.

Burke watched her go, smiling. It was always good to have friends in high places.

A hundred yards up the faint dirt trail, Senator Nolan glanced over at the stocky frame of Colonel David, then around to see where the others were. The giant named

Irons was with the short Sparks woman twenty paces ahead of them on the trail. Lieutenant Burke was at least fifty paces behind them, lugging along the video equipment. The tank crew had remained with their damaged vehicle waiting for help to somehow get it out of the forest.

They climbed a shallow ridge and then started down. She hadn't remembered the trail being this long. She unzipped her ski parka to let the cool morning air in. This mountain was a long way from the busy streets of Washington, D.C.

She pointed ahead down the trail at John Henry Irons. "He sure is one big guy."

Colonel David laughed, the powerful sound filling the forest around them. "He's almost *two* big guys."

"So what's his story?"

"Actually a little unusual, just like the guy. Joined up at seventeen after his parents died. We sent him to college and there he discovered he had a real gift for metallurgy, among many other things. But he really loves the metals."

The senator smiled. "He's got the right name for it. Irons. Right?"

Again the colonel laughed. "Right. John Henry Irons. He did the development for the high-grade alloys we used in constructing those weapons. Without the alloys the weapons wouldn't be possible."

"He's that good, huh?" she asked as she stepped over a small fallen tree.

"Better," Colonel David said. "You ought to see the incredible armor plating he's worked out. And on top of all that he's a good team player."

The senator snorted. "He should've been an NBA player, at his size."

"Yeah," the colonel said. "But Irons said he never had the knack for it. Glad he didn't."

"And Sparks?"

"She's the electronics whiz behind the weapons," the colonel said. "She and Irons make a great team. He designs the weapons, she makes them work, then he comes up with the alloys so that they *will* work."

The senator nodded. "What's the story on Burke?"

"Mostly doesn't fit with this team," the colonel said. "But he's a real genius. And he loves playing with all these powerful high-tech toys we make. He earns his keep by doing all the stuff the rest of us don't want to do."

"Seems a little brash to me," the senator said.

"That he can be," the colonel said. "He's always pushing the envelope."

"Isn't that exactly what you want?"

The colonel laughed again. "Damn right."

CHAPTER 3

THE ABANDONED ADOBE TOWN CLUNG TO THE HOT, dusty desert floor as if a high wind might blow it away at any moment. At one time, back during the boom time of the fifties, this little town had been filled with the sounds of children playing, adults talking, and cars moving along the main street. It had been an alive, growing, western town.

Now a bullet-scarred sign lay facedown in a tumble-weed-filled ditch near the north end of town. Protected from the intense sun, the words on the sign could still be faintly read:

Waterville, Arizona
Population 967

The town had been named back around the turn of the century for a spring that flowed freely from the rock mountainside to the west of the site. Generations of families had been born, raised, and died around the little town, drinking and cooking and growing crops with that steady stream of water. Countless wells punched the dry ground like stab wounds.

Now few even remembered the town, and it had long since disappeared from the modern maps. No children had roamed the streets of Waterville for over thirty years. Like many small towns in America during the fifties and early sixties, the young had moved to the cities, seeing no reason to remain on the family homestead. Then the water table under the desert had dropped and the wells had mostly dried up along with the stream. The last general store and gas station had closed down in 1964 when the freeway was routed thirty miles to the north, ending all the traffic on the old highway.

Now the United States Government owned the town and all the land around it. A high wire fence a mile outside of town kept unwanted civilians from accidentally venturing down the old road and into the remains of Waterville.

Over half of the twenty adobe and wood buildings that lined the main street were nothing more than piles of rubble. Tumbleweeds had formed huge piles against the western buildings, making some of the buildings seem more like small mounds of brush than anything a human had built. The gas station pumps had been removed and the once-bright paint on the buildings had faded to faint, sand-blown memories.

But today, as the afternoon sun sent the temperatures past a hundred degrees, and the hot wind swirled small clouds of dust, Waterville was again filled with some human life.

At two in the afternoon, Colonel David stood in the middle of the old main street, hands on hips, watching as his people finished setting up for the monitoring experiment for the coming weapons tests.

Video and sound stations were placed in two locations, square in the middle of the street like two old gunfighters facing off in a showdown to the death. Two technicians in green Army pants and T-shirts manned each station.

To the right of the colonel was an adobe building that had once been the general store. One flat wall faced the main street. That was to be the target.

Facing the general store was a wooden and concrete building that had been the town's bank. The front window had been completely knocked out, but the building itself seemed solid. It was from inside the bank that they would fire the first tests, as if waiting in sniper mode for enemy soldiers to invade this old ghost town.

Inside the bank, John Henry Irons muscled a sleek electronic gun into an open window, aiming it at the blank wall across the street. He clicked the gun onto a tall tripod stand, then stepped back. He had long before stripped off his camo gear and now wore standard work pants and a tank top. His head and shoulders glistened with sweat. His face was streaked with dirt where he'd wiped away the moisture.

Behind him, Senator Nolan used a handkerchief to keep the sweat off her forehead as she watched the preparations. She had left her ski parka in the truck, and after five minutes of standing in this heat had rolled up the sleeves on her expensive long-sleeved blouse. But even being in the cooler interior of the dusty old bank lobby didn't help much. Between the heat and the thick smell of a building long abandoned, she was far from comfortable.

Sparks and Lieutenant Burke both worked to get recording equipment into place five paces behind where John Henry had placed the gun. Sparks wore a rolled-up T-shirt, stained with sweat, while Burke had taken off his suit jacket, but had kept on his shirt and tie. The white shirt was already streaked black with dirt and huge circles of sweat had formed under his arms.

"This isn't a heat-pulse rifle like this morning, is it?" Senator Nolan asked.

"No, ma'am," John Henry said. "This is a sonic cannon."

Sparks moved up and stood beside the senator.

"This baby," Sparks said, pointing at the gun John Henry worked on in the window, "pumps out an ultra-low-frequency burst of sound energy. It can take out a whole line of troops."

"Without killing 'em," John Henry said, turning to face her. "Just leaves 'em stunned."

"And you like that idea, Mr. Irons?" the senator asked.

"Not killing?" John Henry said. "Yes, ma'am, I have to say I do."

"Set to a higher gain," Sparks said, "it could bring down an entire wall, like the target wall."

"Why not the entire building?" Burke said as he moved up and stood next to the senator.

Sparks snapped around and stared at Burke. "We haven't tested those parameters."

At that moment Colonel David banged through the front entrance, his heavy boots shaking the floor of the old bank. "They're set up in the street. You people ready in here?"

"Ready, sir," John Henry said.

"Ready on the monitoring," Sparks said.

The colonel nodded. "Call it, Sparks."

Sparks flipped up a radio mike from her belt, clicked it on, and said, "This is Little John. Stand by to storm the castle."

John Henry turned and pulled the weapon up into position on the tripod, aiming it at the blank wall of the old general store forty paces away.

"May I do the honors, Colonel?" Burke asked.

The colonel glanced at the senator, then at John Henry, then back at Burke. "I don't see why not."

John Henry hesitated for a moment, then nodded and stepped back, leaving the sonic cannon on its tripod aimed at the far wall. Burke nodded to him and stepped into position behind the cannon.

"Go for it, Burke," the colonel said.

"Gladly, sir," Burke said.

Then Burke glanced at the senator, their gazes locking for a moment.

Quickly, he slid his hand along the barrel of the cannon up to the controls as he worked to line up on the distant wall. Then with a quick flick, he turned the power controls of the cannon up.

Way up.

All the way to the top.

John Henry immediately saw what Burke had done.

"Burke! No!" he shouted and dove toward the lieutenant.

Too late.

Burke fired.

Then the world went into slow motion.

The sound inside the bank was as John Henry had expected of a normal-powered shot. Just a slight smacking sound.

Across the main street Burke's shot made a direct hit on the blank wall with a solid wall of sound. The sonic force seemed to almost lift the building from its foundations.

Then the old store literally imploded, smashing in on itself as if a giant hand had simply crushed it like a wadded-up piece of paper. Part of John Henry's mind recorded all this as if watching it from a distance, while in reality he was still reaching for Burke and the sonic cannon.

Outside, both monitoring teams on either side of the street were tossed backward into the air like dolls, pushed along in the dust and dirt like tumbleweeds before a high wind.

Still in what seemed like slow motion to John Henry, the shock wave bounced back at the bank.

It hit the old bank building with a deafening roar and the impact force of half a dozen bombs.

To John Henry it felt like he had been standing in front of a freight train as it barreled down on him, whistles screaming their full warning.

The unseen force pounded him in a full body smash, pinning him sideways against the side wall of the bank. The impact completely knocked the wind from his chest.

Then the unseen force dropped him to the floor and held him there, like a playground bully standing on his chest.

Burke and the cannon were smashed to the bank floor and pinned there as if the gravity of the planet had suddenly gotten a dozen times stronger.

The colonel was shoved backward away from the front window. He smashed solidly into the old bank cage. It looked to John Henry as if the colonel screamed, but the roaring of the sonic blast covered any noise.

Sparks and the senator were flipped over backward. They both tumbled and ended up against the back stone wall of the building, right under the remains of an old sign that read NEW CUSTOMERS.

John Henry watched, helpless, unable to move, as the wall above them shook and then tipped forward, bringing down the concrete and roof beams in a shower of dust and a huge thundering explosion.

Then it was over.

The sonic wave had passed. Slowly the sounds of the desert returned, mixed with the groaning of building materials settling and the moaning of humans.

The air was choked with dust, and he could barely see to move.

No more than two seconds had passed from the moment Burke had pulled the trigger to the moment the thundering sonic wave had passed.

Two very long seconds that John Henry would remember forever.

"Sparks!" John Henry shouted with what little breath he could manage.

Ignoring the pain in his ribs, he climbed to his feet and in the swirling dust staggered to the huge pile of rubble that had been the back of the old bank.

"Sparks?" he shouted again.

No answer.

"Hold on," he shouted at the huge pile. "I'm coming."

Then with every bit of energy he had in his huge body, he dug into the pile of concrete and wood where he knew his best friend lay trapped.

CHAPTER 4

THE WINDOWLESS COURTROOM SMELLED OF LEATHER and nervous sweat. Outside, the Arizona sun beat down on millions of cars fighting through the Phoenix area traffic, making the afternoon commute a very hot and dangerous one. But inside the courtroom the air-conditioning fought to keep out the heat, sometimes successfully. Sometimes not.

The judge advocate sat behind a slightly raised oak bench facing the moderate-sized room. Chairs filled the back half of the room while an oak rail seemed to cut the room in half. Inside the rail were two tables, one for the prosecution and one for the defense. A six-person all-male jury made up of officers sat to the judge's left.

The two days of proceedings inside the military headquarters had been kept completely quiet from the public. But still a good half-dozen officers with enough security clearance to attend were scattered around the seats, watching.

At the left table sat Lieutenant Nathaniel Burke, his back stiff, his hands constantly moving. A long, obviously fresh red scar cut down Burke's right cheek like a neon strip. It was a mark he would never be able to run from. And never hide.

Beside Burke sat the young-looking Major Gates. Gates had been assigned to represent Burke and for two days had done a fairly good job.

Now halfway through the second day, the court had reconvened after a short lunch recess. The first witness called to the stand was Lieutenant John Henry Irons. He stood solemnly to take his oath, then sat down, his long legs apart, his knees up.

To those watching, his huge frame was an imposing figure filling the front of the courtroom. His presence was almost bigger than his massive frame and his dark eyes seemed to almost control the area around him.

On the outside, John Henry appeared calm and collected, but inside he was shaking, and sweat coated the palms of his hands. He was only a witness. He knew that. He had repeated that to himself over and over. No one had blamed him for what happened. He had tried to stop it. But he was still being asked to recount a day he very much wished to forget.

Major Richards, the lead counsel for the prosecution, stood and faced Irons from a small wooden podium in front of the judge's bench. Richards then spent the next hour grilling John Henry, question by question, to the point in time right after the second arms test in the ghost town and the resulting explosion.

"Mr. Irons," the major said, "when you finished moving the concrete and wooden remains of the bank wall, what did you find under the debris?"

John Henry took a deep breath, then managed to answer calmly, even though the images of that moment were filling his mind like a movie running on fast forward. "I found both Senator Nolan and Lieutenant

Sparks. The senator had been killed outright. Her neck appeared to have been snapped.''

''And Lieutenant Sparks?'' the major asked.

The image of the rubble filled John Henry's mind. He'd thrown off the concrete and lumber like a madman, digging to find Sparks. Then, finally, only one huge piece of concrete remained in his path. Somehow he had managed to lift it and prop it up out of the way with a timber.

Under it was Sparks. Her blood had splattered the concrete and blackened the dust around her. When he lifted the concrete she had managed to smile at him before she passed out.

''Mr. Irons?''

The major's voice snapped John Henry back to the stuffy courtroom.

''I'm sorry, sir,'' John Henry said. ''Would you repeat the question?''

''What was the condition of Lieutenant Sparks?''

John Henry took a deep breath. ''She had a spinal injury and her legs had been crushed by the falling wall. She survived, but she's still in critical condition in intensive care. She's unable to even have visitors. The doctors have told me that she might not walk again, sir.''

A murmur ran through the courtroom as the injuries that John Henry had described sank in.

''Order, please,'' the judge said, then nodded for the major to continue his questioning.

''I can imagine,'' Major Richards said, ''just how difficult these questions are for you.''

''Thank you,'' John Henry said, his gaze focused on the major. ''I'm fine.''

The major nodded and went on, first glancing down at his notes. ''We've heard testimony from Colonel David that you shouted out to Lieutenant Burke to stop just *before* he fired. Is that a correct statement?''

"Yes," John Henry said.

"And *why* did you shout at Burke?"

"The test weapon was calibrated wrong."

"And how was it wrong?" the major asked.

"The intensity level was set at maximum, sir," John Henry said. "Far, far too high."

"A setting that had never been tested or even approved for testing," the major said. "Is that correct?"

"Yes, sir."

"Why was that?" the major asked, staring intently at John Henry. "Who calibrated the weapon? Do you know who set it to maximum?"

The silence in the courtroom seemed to smother any movement, even almost blocking the normal breathing of those watching and waiting for John Henry's answer. Two days of trial, and it had come down to this one question, to this one moment.

John Henry looked directly at Major Richards and then said calmly, "Burke did it, sir."

"You saw him calibrate the weapon?"

John Henry nodded. "As he took over control of the gun he purposely reached forward and slid the calibration to maximum. He knew exactly what he was doing."

Major Richards nodded and stepped away from the podium. "Thank you, Lieutenant. That's all."

Lieutenant Burke glared at John Henry. Then under his breath he said, "It sure as hell is, big guy. Always remember. Payback is hell."

Major Gates glanced nervously at his client and his cold words, then quickly away.

*   *   *

Four long hours later, John Henry and Colonel David left the courtroom, walking side by side through the building's lobby. John Henry's head seemed to almost brush the ceiling. The colonel had to take almost two steps to John Henry's one long stride.

Yet there was no pride to John Henry's posture. He walked like a man beaten and bent over.

The jury had taken almost no time, being out for less than thirty minutes. Guilty. Burke was guilty, something John Henry knew without a doubt. And having a jury agree gave him no joy.

The colonel patted John Henry on the arm. "It's over."

"In more ways than one," John Henry said.

"Look," the colonel said, "you were under oath. You saw Burke do what he did. He's lucky the judge only gave him a dishonorable discharge instead of sending him to Leavenworth."

"Yeah," John Henry said. *"Lucky."*

"Sure as hell hate to lose him, though," the colonel said. "He was one brilliant son of a bitch."

John Henry stopped and glared down at the colonel. "I doubt if Sparks feels the same way, *sir.*"

The colonel nodded, not looking up at the man towering over him. "Well, it's been a damned rotten deal all around. But you'll feel better soon as we get back to work."

"I don't think so," John Henry said.

"Trust me," the colonel said. "We've got a lot to do. We need to assemble a new unit. Press on. We've got a golden opportunity here."

"Opportunity?" John Henry asked, staring down at the colonel as if he'd just actually looked at the man for the first time.

"Look, John, nobody's sorrier than me that people got hurt. But that's the nature of war."

"We're not at war, sir," John Henry said, his voice cold and calm. Then after a few beats he went on. "And the entire idea of these weapons was to stop an enemy without—"

"Without hurting them," the colonel said. "I know. And I know that's why you developed them."

"The only reason," John Henry said.

The colonel looked up at John Henry, his eyes bright with excitement. "John, these weapons are more *powerful* than I ever hoped. C'mon, you saw how those damn buildings folded up. We've created the next generation of weaponry. We can't turn back on that kind of potential firepower."

"Maybe you can't," John Henry said, his voice so cold and angry it rumbled through the lobby. "But after what happened to Sparks, I *can*. Sir."

With that John Henry saluted the colonel, turned and strode through the front door and out into the hot air of the Arizona evening.

CHAPTER 5

THE SMELL OF ANTISEPTIC WASHED OVER JOHN Henry as he pushed through the double doors into the small lobby of the military hospital intensive-care unit. No noise, no music, fought against the heavy silence of the drab room. A few magazines were scattered on a wooden coffee table, and the stained green couches looked cheap and well-worn.

He took a deep breath, shifted the small vase full of flowers to his other hand, and moved quickly to the opposite door of the waiting room.

Pure white and bright fluorescent lights greeted him at the same time as the smell of blood and antiseptic smothered him. He hated hospitals more than any place in the world. He'd wade through a dozen snake-infested swamps before he'd go into a hospital. But Sparks was here.

For Sparky he'd do anything. And she'd finally regained consciousness after almost two weeks.

A thin, dark-haired nurse, busily working on paperwork, ignored him for a moment, then finally stopped and glanced up at him. "You're a big one," she said. "Must be at least six ten if you're an inch."

"Actually seven feet two inches," John Henry said, smiling at her. "Exactly to the inch."

She laughed. "Like I said, you're a big one. Now, what can I do for you?"

"I'm here to see Lieutenant Sparks," he said. "My name is John Henry Irons."

The nurse brightened at his name and came out from behind the desk. "She's been hoping you'd come by since the moment she awoke. But go easy. She's still got a long ways to go."

"Is she still in danger?"

"With as much damage as that woman withstood, there's no telling. But she's awake and getting better, so we're thinking positively."

She pointed at one wide door. "In there."

John Henry nodded his thanks and headed for the door. He tried to prepare himself for what he might see, but over and over the image of Sparks under that concrete kept flashing in his head. It had done that for three weeks now.

He couldn't imagine it ever stopping.

Inside the room he almost didn't recognize his friend. Her bed was surrounded by four large, blinking machines. Wires ran from a dozen places on her body, and tubes bulged from two places under the light sheet that covered her. Her face was a mass of black and blue and her head had been completely shaved. She looked tiny and shrunken lying there. Not at all the robust friend he had known just two weeks before.

"Sparky," he said softly, afraid that by speaking too loud he might hurt her.

For a moment he thought she hadn't heard him. Then her eyelids fluttered and she tried to smile.

He moved up beside her and lightly touched her arm.

"My hero," she whispered, her voice raspy and barely louder than the faint humming from the machines around her.

"These are for you," John Henry said, holding the vase up in front of her to see.

"My favorite," she said.

"No kidding?"

"No kidding," she whispered. Then she slowly brought up her arm and pointed a finger at him.

He smiled and felt an inner flood of relief as he touched his finger against hers in their usual ritual.

She let her arm drop back to her side, then blinked at him, trying her best to look at him. As she did so it was clear that the brain inside that battered body was still working. Slowly life came back into her eyes.

"Civvies?"

"Yeah," he said. "The old street clothes. They feel sort of odd, to tell you the truth."

"So you really did bail, huh?"

John Henry nodded sadly. The feeling of being alone and adrift for the first time in his adult life was very real. He'd been in the service since he was seventeen. He didn't know much else. But it was time he learned. Maybe past time.

"Why?" Sparks whispered.

"My tour was over," he said. "After what happened to you, I ain't planning to go back."

"Well," Sparks said, "I'll come see you, soon as I'm back on my feet."

John Henry nodded. He knew that most likely that would never happen. The doctors gave her almost no chance to ever walk again. But there was no point now in being down around her. She needed his support and he could give it.

"I'm looking forward to that," he said, making his voice sound as light as he could. "And I'm gonna be checking up on you, every week."

He pulled out a card and tucked it under the edge of the vase of flowers on her end table. "There's my address and phone number. You use it, you understand?"

"You still sound like you're in the army," she said.

But under the bruises John Henry could see a slight smile.

"So, civilian," she whispered. "Where are you heading?"

John Henry looked up into the eyes of his best friend. "Home."

She again smiled lightly. "I knew it," she said. "It's about time, I'd say."

He stared at her for a moment, then smiled. "I guess it is."

CHAPTER 6

THE LINCOLN CONTINENTAL RENTAL CAR GLIDED TO a stop against the curb of Ocean Avenue in Santa Monica, California. A line of palm trees, spaced evenly like fence posts, grew out of the sidewalk, forming a line into the distance along the avenue. The sidewalks were clean and the buildings in this area didn't have bars on the windows like most areas of the big city.

On a day like today, only the business people were walking the streets in this area. The summer heat and the blazing sun had forced everyone else down to the beach two blocks to the west in a vain attempt to stay cool.

Beside the car a modest five-story office building filled the block. A flashy, story-high logo blared from one brick wall.

DANTASTIC, INC.

Nathaniel Burke climbed slowly from the Continental and moved around toward the wide glass front door. He

had on a pin-striped business suit and new, highly polished shoes, the best he could afford with his last paycheck from the Army. The red scar cut down his face
like a beacon against his white skin. He still hadn't gotten used to the looks people gave him. The quick stare,
then the even quicker glance away.

He doubted he'd ever get used to it.

But he sure as hell was going to make some people
pay for it. And pay big.

He pulled open the first of the air-lock double doors
leading into Dantastic. A cool air-conditioned draft surrounded him, causing him to break out into a sweat before he had opened the inner door.

Inside, the bright lights and overwhelming sounds of
a hundred video and pinball games forced him to pause.
What would have normally been the lobby was a huge
arcade. Only this was no normal arcade. This lobby was
a business showroom. And a very good one. Salesmen
worked with customers as they looked over the modern
games, playing them, talking about weekly revenues and
average electrical costs.

With a quick look around, Burke headed for the receptionist behind a long black marble counter near the
back of the lobby. She glanced at his scar, then forced
herself to smile at him, looking him directly in the eyes.

"I'm here to see Mr. Daniels," he said, ignoring her
look. "He's expecting me."

Within two minutes Burke was taken up five floors to
a very normal-looking executive office complex filled
with secretaries and copy machines. No flashy games
here.

Just business.

Burke liked that.

The inside of Daniels' office was not so standard. It
was huge even by executive-office standards, with plush

carpets, large paintings, and a sunken living-roomlike area. A gigantic oak desk dominated the area in front of a huge window. The view was to the west, out over the nearby buildings and palm trees to the deep blue of the Pacific Ocean.

Two of Daniels' assistants stood on either side of the big desk. Burke knew them both from his old days in the neighborhood. On the right was a solid-looking woman named Duvray. Burke knew she was Daniels' number one assistant and half ran Daniels' operation. She also was one of the toughest women he'd ever run into, in or out of the service.

She was going to be the biggest problem for him, when the time came. And she would be the first to go when he took over, if she lasted that long.

On the left was a younger man named Singer. Singer had obviously pumped way too many weights and most likely still did. Burke knew that Singer could kill him without even a hint of trouble or remorse. And he would do it at the blink of an eye from his boss, no questions asked.

Burke ignored them as they stared at him.

"How ya doing, Big Willy?" Burke said as the secretary closed the door behind him.

Big Willy Daniels swiveled around in his high-backed leather chair and faced Burke.

Big Willy stood, on a good day, with two-inch heels, maybe five feet. But he was the meanest five-foot human Burke had ever known. And the neatest. Nothing was ever out of place with Big Willy, including the mint toothpick he always seemed to be holding between his lips.

Big Willy's people were always in order, too. You worked for Big Willy and you knew exactly where you stood at all times. Those who didn't weren't around long. Burke had found that out, and he knew it would be Big Willy's downfall.

Big Willy said nothing, only stared at Burke, his cold eyes boring through Burke like a drill.

"Nice setup you got here," Burke said, making a clear gesture to look around without moving from the spot in front of the desk. "Come a long way from the old neighborhood."

Big Willy only nodded, but said nothing.

The two flanking him didn't even blink.

Burke was impressed. Not even the Army had that level of control in its people.

"Word on the street," Burke said, "is you're still dealing hot weapons."

"I distribute arcade games, Burke," Daniels said, his voice much deeper than a man his size would normally have. "I also belong to the chamber of commerce. And I give jobs to a lot of those 'at-risk' kids everyone's always talking about. So I don't know what you've heard, but—"

"I've heard," Burke said, "you'll still sell your mother for a roll of quarters."

Both Duvray and Singer simultaneously took a step forward, but Daniels stopped them with a raised hand. Neither of them stepped back. They only stopped, waiting, like two hungry dogs for permission to feed.

"You come here just to get your ass kicked?" Daniels said, shaking his head at the thought. "Not smart at all, if you ask me. Not like you either, from what I remember."

"Is that any way to treat a man who is gonna make you really big, Willy?"

"You better be talkin' fast," Daniels said, his eyes turning angry.

Burke only smiled. "I'm talking about dealing the

next generation of superweapons. And not just to the crooks and punks on the street, but to the entire damn world.''

Burke stepped closer to the desk.

Both Singer and Duvray made another move toward him, but again Daniels stopped them.

''So what are you after?'' the short man said, pulling the toothpick from his mouth and glancing at it.

Burke laughed. ''Seed money to build the prototypes and do a little, should we say, advertising. We'll be partners in this.''

''So what exactly are you selling?'' Daniels said, leaning forward and staring at Burke.

Burke glanced first at Duvray, then at Singer before slowly pulling a computer disk from his pocket and flipping it in front of Daniels. ''Now that's top secret.''

Big Willy nodded and sat back. ''All right,'' he said. ''We'll talk and look over what you got. But first you tell me how you got the scar.''

Burke laughed, his hand going to the side of his face and the rough skin cutting it in half. Then he looked directly into the cold eyes of Big Willy. ''I got it working on a weapon that will make us rich.''

CHAPTER 7

JOHN HENRY DUCKED HIS HEAD AND CLIMBED DOWN out of the old city bus. The thing had smelled of diesel and vomit and sounded like it might not make it another two miles. And it was the hottest thing he had ever been trapped inside. But for as long as John Henry could remember, the city buses had been like that. And somehow they just managed to keep going.

He swung his duffel over his shoulder as the heat of the afternoon smothered him, coming in waves off the sidewalk. Behind him the door of the bus creaked closed and it lurched off toward its next stop, leaving behind a black cloud.

Around him his old neighborhood shimmered in the hot afternoon sun. Witmer Street.

Home.

The only real home he'd ever known.

Across the street the old Kramer Pharmacy looked to be still in business. Black bars covered its windows and blue and red graffiti covered every inch of the side brick wall. But a new paper sign advertising egg prices hung beside the door. And inside John Henry could see the stooped figure of old man Kramer behind the counter. Sometimes, no matter how much things changed, certain things remained the same.

He could feel the sweat starting to break out on his forehead. A cool glass of lemon tea sounded just fine right about now. He could almost taste it, especially the way Grandma Odessa made it. Actually just about anything she made at this point sounded good.

He turned and headed down the cracked sidewalk of Witmer Street, feeling almost as if he were walking back in time.

Into his own past.

Both sides of the street were lined by trees and parked cars, half of which John Henry doubted had run in years. Small lawns were like light green and brown postage stamps in front of the old brownstones. Most of the buildings needed obvious repairs, and it was clear just from a quick glance that this neighborhood had seen much, much better days.

John Henry didn't remember the neighborhood being this rundown the last time he had come home. Had it been that long? Or had he just not noticed before now?

Maybe now, after what had happened with Sparks, he was just seeing things clearer.

Or maybe just really looking for the first time. He'd have time to figure all that out, now.

He moved down the right side of the street near the old Jennings playground. Five shirtless teenage boys were playing basketball, the netless hoop dangling at a slightly downward angle from the wall. Their yells and grunts filled the air and made John Henry even hotter just looking at them move.

Had he ever been *that* young?

More gang marks covered the brick wall of the park

and the backboard. Near the back corner of the park two younger girls in shorts and T-shirts were jumping rope so fast the rope and their feet were just blurs. He shook his head, marveling at kids and their energy. He couldn't remember ever having that much energy at any age.

On the far side of the street a young woman he didn't recognize pushed a baby carriage toward the pharmacy. She didn't even look at him, almost being *too* careful to not make eye contact.

"Hey, mister," one of the boys yelled. "Ball!"

John Henry turned as the ball rolled toward him from the game. He scooped it up with one hand and held it, his big hands holding the basketball like others would hold a baseball.

"Do it, man," one of the boys said.

John Henry flipped the ball at the hoop, but the ball didn't even come close, bouncing off in the opposite direction as the boys laughed.

John Henry just shrugged and turned to continue down the street. He was tall, but that didn't mean he was good at basketball. That sport took skill and training just like any other, no matter how tall a person was. And he'd just never been interested enough to do the intense work. Now, molding hot metal to do his bidding was much more his style.

"In-com-ing!"

John Henry turned just in time to see thirteen-year-old Martin, his younger brother, rocketing at the corner of the park and the sidewalk on his skateboard, right at where John Henry was standing. The kid wore no shirt and his pants were baggy and drooping so far they looked like they might fall off at any moment. His skin glistened with sweat and health.

John Henry couldn't believe how much the kid had grown. It had been a while since he was home.

Too long.

This time that would change. He was here to stay.

John Henry stepped quickly aside and dropped his bag. With both hands he scooped Martin off the skateboard and swung him around in the air twice to kill the kid's momentum.

He sat Martin down, both of them laughing.

"You'll get hurt like that," John Henry said, "coming in here like some sort of scud."

The boy shrugged. "Nah—you mean stud!"

With a practiced motion Martin moved over and stepped on his skateboard. It flipped into the air in a twirling motion. He caught and tucked it under his arm as if nothing had happened.

"Why you wanna play ya hate me?" he said. "I got all kinds of crazy homies sweatin' me."

John Henry wiped off his hands on his pants, then sniffed them. "Try using a little more dee-o."

Martin smirked. "Yeah. Still corny as hell."

"Nothing changing," John Henry said.

Around the far corner of the park another kid on a skateboard streaked into sight. He was dressed the same as Martin, except that this kid had tattoos on both arms.

It took a moment for John Henry to recognize the kid streaking at them. Lamont Balbum.

Lamont jumped off the board with a few quick running steps and popped fists with Martin.

"What's up, Martin?"

"Peace," Martin said.

Lamont didn't even glance up at John Henry. He just nodded, spun around, and with two swift kicks was speeding away on his skateboard.

John Henry watched him bust through the basketball game and out the other side of the park.

"He can move it," Martin said.

"His brother still locked down?" John Henry asked.

Lamont's older brother was a year younger than John Henry, and had been nothing but trouble for as long as he could remember. The entire Balbum family had been nothing but trouble, and from John Henry's view, Lamont didn't seem to be taking any new course.

"Man," Martin said, laughing, "his brother got more time than a clock."

"And you hang with Lamont?" John Henry asked, obviously already knowing the answer.

Martin dropped the skateboard on its wheels on the sidewalk, then with a kick flipped it back into the air and caught it again. "Nah, I ain't living like that," he said, not looking up at John Henry. "I just be chillin', man. What do you think?"

John Henry looked at the young Martin for a moment, then said, "I think it's good to be home."

CHAPTER 8

THE WONDERFUL SMELL OF SOMETHING BAKING IN the oven greeted John Henry as he opened the front door to Grandma Odessa's brownstone. It was like a warm hand pulling him inside. Instantly his stomach churned and he realized it had been some time since he'd eaten.

"Grandma Odessa!" Martin shouted, jumping around John Henry and dropping the skateboard with a bang on the polished wood floor near the front door. "What up?"

From around the corner of the kitchen door Grandma Odessa appeared, a look of annoyance on her round face. She wore a faded plaid dress covered with a white apron. The apron was stained with brown streaks, and the area of the apron where she rubbed her hands on her wide hips was worn thin.

From John Henry's perspective, Grandma Odessa hadn't changed a bit. She stood no more than five feet tall, and over the years had become almost as round as she was tall. She had a heart of gold, a laugh that wouldn't stop, and a smile that lit up rooms. She was also the best cook John Henry had ever known.

"Shhh!" she said, holding one finger to her mouth and glaring at Martin. "Hush your mouth before you ruin everything."

Martin stepped back. "My bad, my bad," he said, whispering. "But somebody's here to see you."

She glanced up at John Henry.

"Hey, Grandma Odessa," John Henry said in his normal full voice.

"Shhhhhh!" she said, again holding her finger to her mouth. But she was smiling at him.

"What?" John Henry whispered. "What's wrong?"

Grandma Odessa moved up and hugged his middle, which was about as high as she could reach on his tall frame.

He bent over and returned her hug as best he could.

"Oh, Lord," she said, whispering, "how I've missed you, son."

"I've missed you, too, Grandma Odessa," John Henry said, as he hugged her gently back, using the flat of his palms to cover her shoulders. It did feel good to him to be home. And it had been years since Grandma Odessa had hugged him.

She let go of him and stepped away, leaning her head back to look up at him with a serious glare. "You look like you got a little taller."

Then she laughed, shook her head, and turned back toward the kitchen.

John Henry laughed too and glanced at Martin, who rolled his eyes while shaking his head from side to side.

Both of them followed the older woman into the kitchen.

Inside, the warmth and wonderful smells of the white kitchen welcomed John Henry even more. And made him even hungrier.

The old stove still filled a part of one wall next to the new refrigerator he'd bought her a few years back. The wooden kitchen table commanded the area under the window that looked out into the fenced backyard. Sunlight poured in through a second, smaller window over the stained old double sink.

He'd spent many a happy hour in this kitchen. He hoped to spend many more.

Grandma Odessa was on one knee in front of her old stove, peering into the oven.

"Shhh," she said without looking around. "Tiptoe on those size twenty-twos."

She held up her hand to shelter her eyes while she looked into the oven, then she sort of sagged lower to the ground, obviously frustrated.

John Henry glanced at Martin, then at Grandma Odessa. "Can you please tell me what's going on?"

She took an orange knitted pot holder from off its hook beside the stove and opened the oven. She picked out a large bowl and then stood. On a baking sheet she flipped the bowl over, and a large, flat brown mess slid out.

"It's supposed to be a soufflé," she said, staring at it like it might suddenly decide to climb to its feet and jump off the baking sheet.

John Henry managed to not laugh as he moved over and stared down at the ugly mess. "A soufflé?"

Grandma Odessa tossed the orange pot holder onto the top of the stove with a frustrated flip, then shook her head. "It's supposed to be all light and fluffy and full of air. And it *was* until you two came storming in."

John Henry glanced around at Martin, who was slouching in a chair at the kitchen table.

Martin only shrugged.

She nudged the brown mass with one finger, then sighed. "How am I ever going to master the art of French cooking with people crashing in and out all the time like James Brown stomping on a concert stage?"

John Henry glanced down at Grandma Odessa. He wasn't sure he'd heard what she'd said.

"Master the art of—"

Grandma Odessa picked up a book John Henry hadn't noticed spread open on the counter. *The Cordon Bleu.* She held the book up at John Henry. "I'm marrying all my down-home recipes with *haute cuisine*."

She again poked at the brown mess on the stove. "This here was gonna be a hominy soufflé."

Martin snorted. "She wants to open a restaurant. Call it Black and *Bleu*."

John Henry couldn't help it. The laugh burst from his mouth faster than he could move his hand to stop it.

Grandma Odessa glared at him, and he managed to swallow the last part of the laugh, but he knew the grin on his face was far from gone.

Finally he managed to say, "Well, that's a . . ." He hesitated, then added, "Cool name."

"Don't you patronize me, young man," she said, giving him a loving smack on his stomach. "I know where you live. Now, just give me some more sugar."

He laughed again, then reached down and picked her off the ground in a big hug.

She laughed with him, and for the first time since Sparks got hurt, John Henry felt alive again. Coming home had been the right decision. That much was very clear. He didn't know exactly what he was going to do yet, but this was the place to decide.

He sat her down and she straightened her apron, then turned to Martin. "You go finish your studies. I don't want any more of those notes from your teachers."

"Yes, ma'am," Martin said.

John Henry could tell Martin was embarrassed. With only a glance at John Henry, Martin stood and swaggered from the kitchen, banging the wall as he went.

"The gang still trying to get him?" John Henry asked as Grandma Odessa stared at her ruined project again.

"Worse than ever," she said, wiping her hands on her apron and facing John Henry. "It's hard to keep him straight. I'm glad you're back. It will help."

He nodded, but before he could say another thing she continued.

"Now go unpack. And give me your wash. I'll fix you a quick lunch while you get cleaned up." She shook her head at the mess on the stove, then shrugged.

"Oh," she said as he turned to do as she instructed. "There's also a pile of messages for you. I left them on your bed. Who are they, anyway?"

John Henry shrugged. "Job offers, probably. From weapons makers."

Grandma Odessa nodded. "They were all really hot for you."

"They give you any troubles?"

"Nothing I couldn't handle," she said. "You could write your own ticket, though, from the sound of 'em."

She looked up into John Henry's eyes. "Is that why you left the service? To make more money?"

"No," John Henry said, and deep inside he was surprised at how good saying that word felt. "No more weapons. Much better for my soul."

Grandma Odessa stepped over and hugged him around the middle again, then stepped back. "I love you, Johnny."

"I love you, too," he said in return.

"Now," she said, turning back to her mess. "Go unpack if you want something to eat."

Feeling more at home than he had felt in years, he headed for his old bedroom. It felt good to be home.

Really, really good.

CHAPTER 9

THE HUNDREDS OF ARCADE GAMES THAT FILLED THE lobby of Dantastic had become common things for Burke. In the three weeks since Big Willy Daniels had become his partner, he'd been through the lobby full of arcade games a hundred times. Now all the bright lights and salespeople were nothing more than furniture to walk around.

Today was no exception. Burke's mind was a long distance from the commonplace goings-on of people interested in pinball games. Today was the first big test of his new weapon.

He and Big Willy and Duvray moved past the arcade games and into one of the six elevators that serviced the building. Over the last two weeks Duvray had made it clear she didn't much like him. And he'd continued to purposely give her reasons to hate him. She needed to be replaced if what he had in mind with Big Willy was going to work. And she needed to be replaced soon.

Singer, the big muscle-bound bodyguard of Big Willy, was another matter. He could be trained. He had potential.

Burke inserted a special key into the elevator and pushed an unmarked button. In silence the three of them rode toward the basement garage, and then beyond, down two more levels into a secret underground facility.

The doors of the elevator opened on the cold white walls and lab benches that had become a second home to Burke over the last few weeks. The room had a ten-foot ceiling and was divided into three different areas: packing, research, and shooting range. Where better to practice firing guns than sixty feet underground right in the middle of a city?

Six cold-eyed workers labored over arcade game boxes to the right of the elevator in the packing area, slipping and securing AK-47s inside the arcade games, then restoring the games into their shipping crates. An ingenious way to smuggle guns not only across borders, but around the city. No one investigated the interior of locked video games. It just never occurred to the police to do so because most people thought the insides of games were full of electronics and machines. Not so. The electronics took up very little space, so most working pinball games were nothing more than big, empty boxes. Boxes that Big Willy Daniels used to his prime advantage.

Big Willy and Duvray moved over into a Plexiglas-walled monitoring room near the firing range while Burke veered right to a workbench. There he hefted a solid-feeling weapon, slightly longer and fatter than a normal rifle. This was the very thing that would make him rich beyond belief. He loved the feel of it in his hands. It was power, pure and simple.

"All right, Big Willy," he said, turning and holding up the rifle for the short man to see. "As promised, and right on time, the first prototype."

Big Willy pulled the toothpick from his mouth and nodded. "Get on with it."

Burke turned and handed the gun to a red-haired kid named Craig. Burke had used Craig as a gopher over the past two weeks. Good kid. Lots of energy, but almost no brains.

"Don't worry," Burke said. "Just aim and pull the trigger." He pointed down the room at a human-shaped target on the far wall of the shooting range.

Craig nodded and swallowed hard as Burke stepped over to where Big Willy and Duvray stood watching behind an observation shield.

Big Willy glanced up at Burke. "The front office tells me you had a kid you wanted to hire."

Burke nodded, watching Craig start the gun charging. "Just a little personal score to settle."

Big Willy grunted.

Burke glanced down at the little man, keeping his annoyance under control. "Just call it giving back to the community, so to speak."

Big Willy glanced up.

Burke smiled at him. "Surely you understand things like that."

Big Willy chewed on the toothpick and said nothing, simply turning back to watch the test.

"Do it," Burke said to Craig.

The red-haired kid eased the rifle to his shoulder, aimed, and fired at the target.

A bright burst of orange lit up the room as a ball of lightning rocketed out of the muzzle of the gun with a whoosh-bang sound, smashing into the target with a loud smack.

At the same moment a flash also exploded from the breech of the rifle, hitting Craig square in the face.

Craig spun, screamed in pain, and dropped to the

floor, holding his face. The rifle clattered across the concrete floor and Burke moved to pick it up, annoyed at the kid for dropping it.

Duvray quickly moved over and knelt down beside the screaming Craig.

After a second she looked up at Burke. "Jesus! You've burnt half his face off."

Burke just continued inspecting the rifle for damage and for what went wrong.

"Get him upstairs," Duvray shouted to a few of the kids packing boxes. "Call 911 and tell 'em it was an electrical fire."

"Put ice on it," Big Willy said calmly, the toothpick in his mouth moving from side to side.

Duvray helped lift the injured Craig and get him started toward the elevator. Then she came back and faced Burke, her anger boiling very near to losing control. Face-to-face with Burke, she matched his height.

"What are you gonna do about this?" Duvray demanded of Burke.

Burke ignored her and just kept inspecting the rifle for a moment, letting the angry woman stew. Then he held up the rifle slightly. "See this right here," he said, pointing at a place on the breech. "Surge protector needs adjusting."

"I'm talking about him!" Duvray said, pointing at the injured Craig they were just loading onto the elevator. "You nearly killed him, asshole."

Burke shrugged, still looking at the gun. "Had to push the envelope." Then he looked into Duvray's angry face. "And I'm going to remember you called me asshole. It's so original."

Then Burke laughed and turned to go back to the workbench to work on the rifle.

"Mr. Daniels," Duvray said to Big Willy. "This guy's a nut case. Let me—"

Big Willy pointed down the target line. "Duvray, look at the target."

Duvray glanced around as Big Willy indicated. Burke knew exactly what the angry woman was seeing. The target was almost nonexistent. A few shreds of it were still hanging on the wall, but the rest was nothing but litter around the floor. Except for the little problem with the adjustment, the test had been a complete success.

Big Willy turned to Burke, chewing on his toothpick. "Keep up the R and D, Burke."

"Second test tomorrow," Burke said.

Big Willy nodded and without another word headed for the elevator chuckling to himself.

Duvray took two quick steps to a position near Burke. Then she hissed at Burke, "Accidents could happen to you, pal."

Then she spun and moved after Big Willy.

Burke just watched her go, a very cold, very confident smile on his face.

CHAPTER 10

JOHN HENRY WALKED THROUGH THE STEEL MILL, smiling to himself. The incredible noise around him was muffled by the earplugs in his ears. Glowing sparks from the hot steel shot in all directions from one forge as he walked past, but he ignored them, his shift over. A phone call to Sparky, pick up his paycheck, and then home to a wonderful dinner cooked by Grandma Odessa. This was the life he'd hoped for, dreamed about.

The only thing that would make it better was having Sparks closer.

His muscles were coated with sweat and his shirt clung to his back. But even after a long hot day of work he still felt good. Two weeks now of working on the line at the steel mill. Two weeks of back-breaking labor. Two weeks of hard work that he had enjoyed more than he would have imagined possible.

Just working with metal in its raw state pleased him. His degree and experience with metals and making guns had brought him dozens of job offers, but he'd turned them all down to take this one. It wasn't at the level he'd got to work at in the service. Not by a long, long ways, but he also wasn't making guns. He'd checked. Not one scrap of the metal from this plant went to arms manufacturing. And for the moment that was all that was important.

That, working with metal, and being home again.

He moved into the employee lounge. Ten long tables filled the fluorescent-lit room. Twenty food and pop vending machines lined one long wall like soldiers standing at attention waiting for orders. Signs covered the walls shouting out information on a dozen topics from labor meetings to cleaning up your own mess.

A half-dozen other workers were sitting around the room, most likely waiting for their paychecks. He nodded to a few of them he knew from the line, then moved to the pay phone and punched in a long number.

Behind him a number of the women started whispering to themselves quietly. John Henry didn't realize it, but he was the talk of the mill. Every woman in the place seemed to have a crush on him.

And he hadn't noticed one of them. Not one. And that made him even more desirable.

But he had no idea of the conversation going on behind him as he stood facing the phone, waiting.

After two rings the phone on the other end was picked up.

"VA Hospital," a woman's voice said.

"Lieutenant Susan Sparks," he said.

There was a long pause. Longer than John Henry knew was normal for connecting to Sparky's room.

"I'm sorry," the woman said after almost thirty seconds. "We have no one by that name here."

John Henry felt his stomach twist into a tight knot. What could have happened? She had been recovering at a good pace the last time he had called her a week ago.

Did she suddenly die and no one told him? He forced the thought down below the surface and made himself think.

"Ma'am," he said, swallowing a large gulp of air and forcing himself to stay calm. "She was there just a week ago. Would you please check to see what happened to her?"

"Hold on a minute," the woman said and the phone went quiet again. Not even music filled the emptiness he held to the side of his head.

And nothing would fill the hole in his chest if Sparky wasn't there.

John Henry forced himself to take a deep breath and let it out. The images of Sparks under that wall, her blood everywhere, filled his mind again. He wasn't responsible. He'd told himself that a hundred times, but so far he wasn't convincing himself at all.

He doubted he ever would.

"Paycheck," a woman's voice said behind him, breaking the images of that horrible day that had played out like a nightmare, only in full daylight in the heat of the Arizona summer.

He turned around and smiled as best he could at her. "Thanks," he said as she handed the envelope to him. Then he turned back to the silent phone.

Behind him the woman sighed. Just like every woman around the mill, the big, good-looking guy hadn't paid her any attention. Maybe next time. She could only hope.

On the phone the woman at the VA Hospital came back on the line. "Sir, Lieutenant Sparks has been transferred to St. Louis. Would you like the number?"

"Please," John Henry said.

Then, with his heart slowly calming and his breath returning to some sort of normal in-and-out cycle, he wrote Sparky's new telephone number on the back of his paycheck.

CHAPTER 11

DUVRAY MOVED BRISKLY FROM HER OFFICE NEXT TO Big Willy Daniels toward the elevators. Daniels was already gone and had been most of the afternoon. All she wanted to do was get home, take a long cool shower, and then get back down to the club for the night. She hadn't been out on the town for almost a week and tonight she was hot and ready for just about anything that wore tight pants, smiled, and managed to keep up with her.

She noticed that in the lobby outside the executive suite Singer stood at the elevator with two others, waiting. She nodded to him and he smiled back. There had been times she'd wondered what Singer did after work, but she'd never asked him. From the looks of his huge arms and muscles in his neck, most likely he spent the evenings in a gym, pumping iron.

And even though he was a fairly good-looking man, she had never once thought of him as a take-him-home-and-do-it type of guy.

She turned to face the elevator, her thoughts turning to the wonderfully cool shower waiting for her.

*   *   *

Burke smiled to himself. He had stood waiting just inside the emergency staircase off the upper lobby, watching through a small crack in the door. He'd been standing in there for the last twenty minutes.

Waiting for Duvray.

When he saw her appear he said softly, "Got ya."

Then when she turned her back to face the elevator he moved into the room and toward those waiting as if he'd just come from somewhere in the main offices.

He smiled at Singer, then turned and smiled as big as he could at Duvray.

Singer nodded. "Burke." Singer's eyes were friendly and always had been, almost from the first week. It was as if he knew Burke was going to be in charge and he'd better be nice. Duvray on the other hand wasn't that smart.

She just glared at Burke's smile for a moment, then looked away. For the past week since the accident on the first test, she'd done nothing but undercut him. But now, tonight, right here in the office, that would end.

The elevator door slid open with a soft *ding*.

Burke smiled to himself. He had blocked the other two elevators from coming up this far. This one only went as far down as the lower parking garage. Perfect for what he had in mind for Duvray.

She stepped on, followed by two office workers Burke didn't know. Too bad for them.

Singer stepped forward. Burke hesitated, then followed closely behind the big guy. No point in letting him go out with Duvray. He'd come in handy in the future.

As Burke stepped past the edge of the elevator door he stopped, making sure the door remained open.

"Damn. Forgot something," he said, as if to himself.

He glanced up at the big man. "Hey, Singer, give me a hand, will you?"

The big man nodded and stepped back off the elevator with Burke.

As the doors slid closed, Burke caught Duvray's cold gaze as she stood facing the door.

He smiled and waved good-bye.

The glee was almost more than he could contain.

Instantly Duvray knew something was wrong. Maybe it was the satisfied look on Burke's face. Maybe she was imagining that, but she doubted it. She just felt something was wrong, and she'd learned a long time ago to go with that feeling.

Instantly.

Then face the problems later. Such action had kept her alive a number of times in the past.

She stepped forward and hit the red stop button on the elevator panel.

Nothing happened.

With an unusual hard clank the elevator started down.

"Shit! Shit! Shit!" she yelled as she punched the stop button on the elevator, without success.

Outside the elevator in the executive-floor lobby Burke reached into his pocket and pulled out a small black remote-control device. Without Singer noticing what he was doing, he smiled and punched one button twice.

In the elevator motor room above the top floor there was a high-voltage flash, followed by the sound of metal tearing and exploding. The sound echoed through the building like an earthquake.

"Did you hear that?" Singer said.

"I sure did," Burke said.

The smell of burning electrical wires quickly filled the

lobby around Burke and Singer. For a moment it felt as if the entire building had been hit with something large from above.

Then it stopped as suddenly as it started and only the smoke remained.

"What happened?" Singer said, his gun drawn as he quickly scanned the lobby.

Above them the elevator cable motor spun with a high-pitched whine, wildly out of control, smoke pouring from the entire mechanism.

On the elevator Duvray slammed her fist into the elevator's control panel as the elevator jerked and then started dropping toward the basement.

Her weight went to nothing as she hit free-fall. She braced herself against the railing on the side and tried to lift her foot up to kick the panel.

The two others on the elevator screamed.

And screamed.

And screamed.

She didn't.

She knew exactly what had happened.

Clear to the bottom she yelled, "Burke! Burke! Burke!" as she slammed the elevator control panel over and over, as if the panel were his face.

The elevator hit the solid concrete bottom of the shaft after falling seven floors.

The center elevator door on the lower parking garage suddenly exploded outward as if a bomb had been set off behind it.

Parts of Duvray and the other two passengers were scattered over the garage floor like spatter-paint over a smooth, new board.

It would take the police two hours just to determine how many were on the elevator.

In the executive office suite lobby, Singer and Burke both stood staring at the incredible noise coming from the elevator. Singer seemed to be in shock.

He turned to Burke. "What . . . what happened?"

Burke shook his head. "Sounds to me as if the elevator broke loose and dropped to the basement."

"Duvray?" Singer said, staring at the closed door.

"Most likely dead," Burke said, patting the big man on the back.

"Lucky you called me back," Singer said, staring at Burke.

Burke laughed softly. "That it is," he said. "And I need someone I can trust now that Duvray is out of the way. Is that you?"

Singer glanced at the elevator, then back at Burke. Then slowly he seemed to understand. With another quick look at the closed elevator door he smiled and nodded.

"Good," Burke said, patting him on the back again. "Very good choice."

CHAPTER 12

T HE INSIDE OF THE POLICE CAR SMELLED OF DISIN-
fectant and Norma's light perfume. Vanilla mixed
with roses. John Henry enjoyed her smell. Over the
years he'd forgotten how much he liked Norma. And
how much he hated being inside normal-sized cars. Even
when sitting sideways slightly in the front seat of the
police car he had to slouch to keep his neck straight
under the roof of the car. Give him an open-air motorcycle anytime. Lots of head room out there.

Beside him Norma had her jet-black hair tucked up
under her policewoman's hat, and her nightstick lay on
the seat between them, tucked against her hip. Her eyes
mostly stayed focused on the road as she drove, but
every so often she'd glance his way with a bright smile.

Behind them Martin rode in the back, almost as much
a prisoner to the ride as if he'd been arrested. This town
hall meeting was the last place he'd wanted to go. And
he'd made that very clear to both John Henry and
Grandma Odessa. Not even riding in the back of
Norma's police car had changed his bad mood. Might
even had made it worse.

John Henry had been home now almost three months and working at the steel mill for over two. He had called Sparks every week, but nothing seemed to cheer her up at all. And from what the nurses had told him, she wasn't getting much better.

Mostly during the last two months he had focused on being home with Grandma Odessa and Martin. But the longer he was home, the more disturbed he had gotten about the direction Martin was heading. And nothing he'd said so far had changed anything. Maybe tonight might help.

Norma swung the car over one lane and stopped at a red light on the corner of Fourth Street. She glanced at John Henry, a slight twinkle in her eye. "Remember the last time we were in a car together?"

John Henry laughed softly. "Not likely to forget that night. Not likely at all." Just the memory of that night along with the familiar smell of her perfume made him feel young again. As if all those years in the service hadn't happened.

She laughed with him. "Wasn't the front seat, was it?"

"Wasn't a cop car, either."

She laughed and he reached over and patted her hand warmly. Their gazes held for a short moment as the warmth of her hand felt good against his. Then the light changed to green and she returned both hands to the steering wheel.

John Henry actually felt disappointed. Norma was the first woman to interest him since he'd gotten home. And besides her being a cop, he didn't know much about her life.

"Norma, what's with this *town* meeting?" Martin said from the back seat. "Sounds whack."

Norma smiled and glanced in the mirror at Martin. "It

could help get the new antigang program set up. I thought you two might share some insights.''

She glanced at John Henry with a slight smile, then turned to look at Martin over her shoulder. ''Maybe even learn something.''

She turned back to her driving.

Again John Henry reached over and patted her leg in a thank-you motion where Martin couldn't see.

''Why learn when I can earn?'' Martin said. ''One of my homeys snagged me to work at a place called Dantastic. They sell those bomb arcade games!''

John Henry turned so he could see Martin. ''That's what I'm talking about. Get away from those knuckle-heads and into something legit.''

Martin sat up in the back seat. ''So that means I don't have go to this meeting, right?''

John Henry laughed. ''Wrong.''

Martin slouched down as Norma patted John Henry's hand this time.

CHAPTER 13

THE GUN-METAL GRAY OF THE ARMORED HUMMER seemed to suck the light out of the very air around it. Burke stood to one side with Big Willy Daniels and admired his handiwork. The world had never seen a vehicle like this one.

Ever.

The entire shell of the Hummer had been replaced with special alloy metal siding that would stop just about anything fired at it. A dozen high-powered, shatterproof lights were arranged around the front and the tires were made of a special antipuncture material and framed with alloy shields around them.

The front window was covered with metal strips to block all but the luckiest shot, and the front and side windows were of the best bulletproof glass Big Willy's money could buy.

But the best features were the guns. Mounted inside the back side window of the armored Hummer was a very special sonic cannon. A sonic cannon more powerful and more refined than the one that had knocked the wall down and scarred his face.

Mounted to the top of the Hummer's roof was a laser cannon that could cut through steel like it didn't exist. With a simple swipe that laser cannon could cut an entire car in half.

This Hummer was the most powerful land vehicle ever seen. And soon the world would know about it.

Burke moved with Big Willy over to the Hummer where Singer lay on the front floor, his head under the dashboard, his feet dangling out the side door as he finished a minor adjustment.

"Your new recruits together?" Burke asked.

Singer slid out from under the dashboard and sat up. "We're ready to start kicking ass," he said.

Burke turned to Big Willy, who only nodded.

Burke patted Singer on the shoulder. "Show the world what we got."

Singer smiled. "With pleasure."

Thirty minutes later the armored Hummer turned the corner onto Sixth Street, moving steadily and with a low rumble. The entire two blocks were deserted except for a homeless man sitting against one wall half a block down.

The Hummer rolled up to a position directly in front of the Compubank front entrance. The bank was a two-story California-style building, with huge glass front windows and adobe-looking sides. Inside, the night lights showed a half-dozen desks, a wooden counter, and a steel vault in the back.

Singer turned from the steering wheel in the faint light inside the Hummer. Five kids were behind him, all trying not to look worried. They were members of a local gang and he'd trained them himself for this mission.

"Get ready," he said. "Guns charged and armed."

Then he turned back to face forward. "Looks clear, Burke," he said.

On the small screen on the dashboard Burke nodded.

Burke was back at what he called "Control," monitoring everything around the Hummer, as well as all police bands.

"Everything on the monitors seems clear from here," he said. He glanced at Big Willy, then turned back to the screen and Singer. "Do it."

Singer glanced over his shoulder to the kid at the side window. "Blow it."

The side port of the Hummer hissed open and the muzzle of a large weapon appeared.

A sonic cannon.

The gun fired.

Inside the Hummer there was a slight concussion that Singer could feel in his ears, but nothing more.

Instantly the glass and front wall of the bank shattered, then collapsed in a roar. The sonic burst had ripped it apart like a child tearing down a stack of toys.

A half block up the street the homeless man tumbled head over heels at the force of the explosion. Dozens of other windows smashed apart along the street.

Building and car alarms went off everywhere, filling the night air with a sound that demanded attention.

The laser cannon on the Hummer turned and aimed at the bank vault, now clearly exposed to the street and the warm night air. The bright red beam struck out with a sharp hiss, cutting into the metal of the vault right above the lock.

A patch of the vault door instantly melted and dripped to the floor like colored water as the laser cut effortlessly through the locking area.

The side and rear doors of the armored Hummer hissed open. Five gang members in black jumpsuits and hoods leaped from the vehicle and rushed over the remains of the bank's front wall toward the vault.

"Watch out for the hot shit on the floor," one said, pointing to the cooling metal.

Working for the moment as a unit, they got the vault door swung open.

Then, as they saw the inside of the vault, all signs of discipline broke down.

They shouted.

They yelled.

They leaped in the air as if their favorite team had just won the world championship.

Inside the vault, money was everywhere. Some of it stacked, some of it bagged. They had never seen so much money in one spot before and the sight made them crazy.

They rushed inside and scooped the money into their arms.

"One sack each," Singer said, his deep voice clear through the communicators they wore in their ears under their hoods.

Two of them instantly picked up a sack and turned for the door.

The other three paid no attention to Singer.

Outside, another sound filled the canyon between the buildings, joining the bank and other building alarms echoing down the street. Cop car sirens.

"Three cop cars almost at your position," Burke said to Singer. "Clean this up."

Singer flicked on the mike for the kids in the bank. "One bag each. Cops on the way. Out of there. *Now!*"

Down the street in front of the Hummer a cop car slid around the corner and came to a stop in the middle of the street, its red and blue lights flashing off the broken glass that filled the street.

Singer laughed, staring at it. "This is going to be fun," he said to himself. "A lot of fun."

CHAPTER 14

JOHN HENRY HAD LET HIMSELF RELAX FOR A MOment with Norma. She was driving and her faint perfume kept reminding him how much he really had enjoyed her company before he joined the service. Maybe they could get together again sometime, on a more personal basis.

Behind him, in the back seat of the patrol car, Martin slouched, not saying anything. John Henry could tell that going to this antigang meeting was the last thing Martin wanted to do. But wanting to do something and needing to do it were two different things. Martin *needed* to go to this meeting.

Suddenly the police radio blared to life, filling the air between John Henry and Norma with its urgency.

"All units in the vicinity," the woman dispatcher said, "possible 211 in progress. 2218 Sixth Street."

Norma grabbed the mike on her radio instantly. "Three Adam Six. I'm three blocks away and on it. Request backup."

In one smooth and obviously practiced motion she

replaced the mike in its holder on the front of the radio, then hit a button to start the siren and another to start the flashers.

The sound of the siren filled the patrol car as the radio blared response after response to the call.

"Hang on," Norma said.

The police car surged forward as Norma used both hands to swerve the vehicle through a hard right corner.

John Henry knew exactly where they were heading. The address given was his bank. But how was someone robbing a bank at night? Most likely this was nothing more than a janitor setting off an alarm. At least he hoped that was the case.

"Yeah!" Martin yelled as he suddenly sat up straight, holding onto the back of Norma and John Henry's seat. "That's what I'm talking about. Let's get ready to rumble."

John Henry didn't say a word, just kept his gaze glued to the road in front of them as Norma expertly cut the patrol car down a narrow side street and past two slow cars. She was one fine driver. Best John Henry had seen in some time.

Within another ten seconds she spun the patrol car sideways onto the corner of Sixth Street and came to a stop facing another patrol car across Sixth, stopped on the other corner.

What John Henry saw in front of the bank shocked him.

The entire front of the bank had been blown completely away. He could hear the bank's alarm and about a dozen other building and car alarms filling the street with noise over the top of the police sirens.

The other patrol car had arrived a few moments ahead of Norma and two officers were already piling out of the car, guns drawn.

In front of the bank sat a gray vehicle. It looked military in nature, with armor covering every inch of its sides. A large gun seemed to be mounted on the roof. Two doors in the vehicle were wide open, and four men dressed in black were scrambling over the rubble that was all that remained of the front of the bank.

All four of them carried large weapons and sacks, and were heading at top speed for the strange vehicle.

The two cops on the other side both ducked down behind their car, guns aimed at the fleeing robbers.

Suddenly one of the robbers stopped, turned, and fired at the cops.

Bursts of ball lightning smashed into the side of the car, sending electricity crackling through the air. Blue electrical bolts wrapped the police car like a hand grabbing a baseball.

Ball lightning!

John Henry couldn't believe his eyes. What kind of weapon were they using? The only weapons he knew that fired that type of charge were the ones he'd helped develop. And those were top secret. No way bank robbers could get copies of them. Most of the top brass in the Army didn't even know such weapons existed.

The robber fired again and two more pulses of lightning smashed into the patrol car, kicking it up and backward a good three feet. Both officers tumbled head over heels out onto the street.

"Martin!" John Henry shouted. "Stay in here and down until I get back!"

He leaped out of the patrol car at the same moment Norma grabbed her radio.

"Officers down at 2218 Sixth!" she shouted into the mike. "We got big problems here! Requesting backup."

Martin climbed out of the back seat as John Henry

crouched as low as he could and moved across the street toward the downed officers.

Norma finished calling for help as the four thieves piled into the van. The armored vehicle was pointed in her direction.

She quickly gunned the patrol car, sliding it around sideways, blocking the middle of the road with the car. Then she scrambled for the passenger door, to crawl out on the side of the car away from the robbers.

She didn't make it.

Inside the armored Hummer, Singer shook his head as the patrol car blocked his path. "Not a good move at all, sugar," he said.

With a quick twist of a knob he aimed the cannon on the roof. Then with a flick he punched the trigger.

The Hummer rocked slightly and a rumbling boom covered all the siren and alarm noise.

A huge tidal wave of sonic force smacked broadside into Norma's patrol car, flipping it over like a matchbox toy in a child's hand.

On the sidewalk Martin was knocked flat with the force, but not harmed.

Norma's patrol car, shoved by the unseen force, sheered off a fire hydrant, sending a geyser of water into the air.

Two other parked cars behind Norma's patrol car were flipped over as her car skidded on its roof and smashed into the side of a brick wall, coming to rest half on its roof, half on the driver's side.

John Henry had just made it to the downed officers when the blast hit Norma's car.

He stood. "Norma!"

The doors on the armored vehicle in front of the bank

slammed closed and the tires spun as it roared down the street, right past John Henry. It turned a hard right and was gone.

John Henry made it to Norma's car in twenty long, running strides, the last three through the spraying hydrant water.

"Fire!" Martin said, pointing to the engine of Norma's upside-down car. "Johnny, there's fire!"

John Henry glanced at where Martin had pointed. The engine had caught fire and the smell of spilled gasoline was everywhere.

"Stay back, Martin," John Henry shouted.

This time Martin did as he was told, moving a step back and against a brick building.

John Henry quickly moved around to the front of the car and got down to look through the spider-web pattern of the shattered front window.

He could see Norma through the glass, but she wasn't moving. And he couldn't tell if she was breathing.

He quickly moved around to where the car was braced against the wall. With all his strength he braced himself against the wall and shoved the car, skidding it two feet over the pavement away from the wall.

It was just far enough to let the car drop down on its top.

Quickly he used one hard kick to smash the driver's side window.

Then as carefully as he could, he pulled Norma through, picking her up as if she were nothing more than a child's doll.

Cradling the woman, he ran toward Martin just as the patrol car exploded.

The concussion smashed into his back and a small piece of glass nicked him in the arm, but he kept his balance.

A moment later he placed Norma beside one of the other injured patrolmen.

Her eyes fluttered and she opened them.

"Rest," he told her, putting a hand gently on her shoulder so that she wouldn't move. "Help's on the way."

Then he remembered the last time he had said those exact words: to Sparks.

Moments after he had lifted a concrete wall off her crushed legs.

The shock of the memory and the repeated words caught the breath in his throat and twisted his stomach into a sick knot.

Not again.

It couldn't happen again.

But it just had.

CHAPTER 15

SINGER SWUNG THE HUMMER AROUND THE CORNER like it was a race car and he was in the final lap of the Daytona 500. The shocks kept the armored hum-vee solid and almost level. For such a big, heavy beast, the thing handled real well.

And the job had gone off like a charm. The sonic cannon had done exactly what Burke claimed it would do. The front of that bank had just crumbled like a dry cracker, and that cop car had flipped over like a piece of paper in the wind.

On the video monitor on the dashboard, Burke was even smiling. And Burke didn't smile that often unless he wanted something. This time his smile was a satisfied one.

Behind him, the kids who had piled into the Hummer were untangling themselves after his fast takeoff and sharp corner had sent them tumbling into a huge pile, bags of money and all.

Now they had sorted themselves out.

Suddenly Slats, the leader of the gang, shouted to Singer. "Hey man, Cutter ain't here!"

"What?" Singer said. On the monitor it was clear that Burke had heard.

Singer glanced around at the four in the back. There should have been five. "Where the hell is he?"

Slats shook his head. "Man, he was with us in the vault."

"Maybe he cut," one of the others said.

"Shit! Shit! Shit!" Singer said, pounding his hand over and over on the steering wheel.

"Find him," Burke said from the monitor, his voice cold and very controlled. "That gun he's carrying can't get out. Kill him if you have to. Hold on."

On the screen Burke reached forward and punched a few buttons, then studied something for a moment before looking back into the camera. "He's just leaving the bank area and moving down Sixth toward the rail yard. Get to him before the cops do. Understand?"

Singer nodded. Burke must have had tracking devices installed in all the guns. Smart.

With a sure move Singer swung the Hummer around and headed in a new direction. If Cutter had decided to go on his own toward the rail yard, Singer knew exactly where he would go. And Singer would be waiting for the stupid kid.

And Singer's smiling face would be the last thing the kid would ever see.

John Henry kneeled over Norma on the sidewalk, the pain showing clearly on her face in the orange light of the car fire. She had some bad cuts and bruises, but it looked like she was going to be all right.

"Johnny," Martin shouted over all the noise from the bank and car alarms. He grabbed John Henry's shoulder and pointed at the bank.

John Henry looked up in time to see one of the rob-

bers in the black jumpsuits sprint out of the bank, over
the pile of rubble in front of the bank, and up the street
away from the police cars. And he was carrying one of
the rifles that had fired the electrical charge.

"Oh, it's on now!" John Henry said, low and mean.
Then he turned to Martin. "Look out for Norma until I
get back."

Martin nodded.

With a sure move John Henry was on his feet and
running, letting his long legs stride out, covering huge
chunks of ground with every running step.

He was beyond mad. He could feel his blood pumping
and his breath coming hard and that just made him angrier and angrier.

The robber cut up a city block, over a fence and under
a freeway underpass, running like a deer being fired on
by a bunch of hunters.

But John Henry was gaining on him.

The robber was fast, but not anywhere near as fast as
a giant angry man who knew how to run. John Henry
knew how to run. And he was in Army-shape and very
angry.

The images of Sparks and Norma, both injured,
swirled through his mind and spurred him even faster.

The robber went down an alley and over a chain-link
fence, scrambling like he was trying to run in the air.

John Henry hit the fence as the kid splashed down
into a puddle on the other side, then headed off.

John Henry remembered from basic training exactly
how to scale a fence or wall. With two quick pumps of
his legs he was on his stomach on the top metal bar of
the fence. He used his upper body to lever his lower legs
up and over. With a quick twist and release, he dropped
lightly to the concrete on the other side.

Then almost without breaking stride he was headed after the robber. He had gained ground.

The robber had now lost his black hood. John Henry could tell the robber was young, most likely one of the gang members. A purple bandanna flapped around his neck as he ran.

He was also carrying a very modern-looking rifle of some sort. John Henry very much wanted to see exactly what kind it was.

There was a tall, barbed-wire-topped gate at the end of the alley. The robber slid quickly between the edge of the gate and the brick wall of the building, then ran on.

But John Henry was too big to get through that way. Using the gate as a leverage, he quickly climbed up the wall, over the edge of the wire and then down the other side. But now he'd lost some of the distance he'd gained on the first fence.

Ahead of him the robber was trying to maneuver the rifle off his shoulder as he ran, but was having no luck.

John Henry made note of that fact. The kid wasn't trained.

Ahead the rail yard loomed, the sounds of locomotives moving freight cars screeched and ground in the night.

The kid scaled the wire fence into the yard with a quick climb, and John Henry went over behind him even faster.

There had to be two dozen tracks filled with freight cars at this point in the yard. The kid scrambled over a gravel pile and headed toward the cars along the top of a long pile of dirt.

"Hey!" a lineman shouted at the kid, who was running at him. The guy must have been up on the pile of dirt to see out over the cars. "We're switching! You'll get killed out there."

John Henry watched as the lineman moved to stop the running kid.

The kid in one quick move slammed into the lineman.

The guy went over backward, tumbling down the slope and out onto the closest track.

The kid kept moving down the ridge of dirt while John Henry veered down toward the lineman. Like picking up a child, he hefted the lineman in his arms, stepped to the side and laid him down off the tracks on the side of the hill.

The guy moaned and his eyes flicked open.

"You all right?" John Henry asked.

The guy nodded, his eyes clearing.

"Take it easy for a minute," John Henry said. "I'm going after the kid."

With a sure running jump he cleared the first set of tracks and headed down the lines between boxcars. The kid was nowhere to be seen, but if John Henry guessed right, the kid wouldn't go out into the cars too far. He'd stay along the edge and find cover.

Ten cars down the line his guess confirmed itself.

A burst of ball lightning smacked into the boxcar five feet behind him. The force of the blast sent him tumbling.

He rolled twice and came up behind the wheels of an empty boxcar, their protection between him and the direction the shot had come from.

Now what?

Suddenly the world around him seemed to explode and pain shot through his ears as he was flipped over into the dirt.

His mind knew what had happened. He'd been hit by

a sonic blast. The only thing that saved him was the boxcar.

But the boxcar seemed to have a life of its own. It shook, lifted slightly, and then started to tip over.

Right on top of him.

"Shit!" he said as the wall of wood came rushing down at him. But again his service training took over. He rolled sideways toward the center of the car just in time to be in the exact place where the boxcar's open side door was located.

The boxcar smashed down around him, shaking the ground like a bad earthquake.

Everything went black as the impact of the car filled the air with clouds of dirt and dust.

But nothing actually hit him.

He lay still for a moment in the darkness, hoping the dust would settle. And slowly it did. But the blackness remained.

Slowly he stood, then reached up about a foot and touched the wood above him. He was inside an over-turned boxcar that smelled of cattle.

Above him the door was closed.

And locked.

CHAPTER 16

ON THE SCREEN IN THE DASHBOARD OF THE HUM-
mer, Burke was swearing continuously, as if there
were no other words. Finally he addressed Singer.
"That idiot kid of yours has fired the rifle, *my* rifle,
twice."

"Shit," Singer said. Burke had given them clear in-
structions. The guns weren't to be fired except near the
bank in their escape. And then only if needed. Now Cutter had split on them and was running through the neighborhood firing at who knew what.

"He's at the edge of the rail yard, just off Tenth
Street," Burke said.

"Almost there," Singer said.

"Get that gun," Burke said. "It will be my decision
when the punks of this neighborhood get these weapons.
And not one moment before."

Singer said nothing.

John Henry used his foot to kick a hole in what had
been the roof of the boxcar, then crawled through and

out into the light of the rail yard. If he was lucky, the kid thought he was dead. And he'd just let the kid think that for a few minutes longer.

He quickly ran down the line of boxcars to his right. If he figured right, the kid would stay hidden for a few minutes, waiting to see if John Henry was moving, then he'd head back into the city. John Henry's plan was to be there when the kid moved.

He ran past ten boxcars, then ducked between two and up the slight incline to the fence and the street beyond. With a quick climb and roll he was over and across the street, his back against the hard bricks of the building.

The shots had come from the remains of an old building a block up the street and just inside the rail yard fence. John Henry hoped the kid was still hiding in there. If he was he was watching the other direction and would never expect John Henry to be waiting for him out here.

John Henry moved quickly along the wall to a place in an alley just across from the building.

Then, hiding in the shadows, he saw movement from the old shack.

The kid came out, still carrying the rifle. Only now he wasn't wearing the black jumpsuit.

The kid ducked through a hole in the fence, glanced up and down the street, and then headed for the alley where John Henry hid.

John Henry waited until the kid had entered the alley, then stepped from the shadows and grabbed the rifle from the kid's hands in one quick move.

The kid was yanked off his feet. He landed hard and flat on his back on the concrete. The smacking sound echoed through the alley.

John Henry glanced down at the weapon in his hand, then almost dropped it. No way could he be holding what he was holding. It was a Model 3.5 Sonic Rifle, one of the most top-secret guns in the service.

One of the guns he had helped create.

The kid on the concrete sat up, then stood quickly when he saw John Henry with the gun.

"Back up off me, man," he said, his hands up. "Don't get smoked, now."

John Henry swung the barrel of the gun around until it pointed at the kid. Then he took a step forward, his anger barely controlled.

"Where did you get *this*?" he said, spacing each word as if it were a separate sentence.

"I found it, fool!" the kid said.

"Found it," John Henry said, his voice low and cold and beyond anger. "You don't tell me where you *found* it, you'll *find* my fist in your mouth. And you'll *never* find your teeth again."

John Henry could feel the weapon shake in his hands as he gripped it so hard his anger showed.

Suddenly a man stepped from the shadows down the alley, rifle aimed at Cutter and him.

Before John Henry could react, a ball of lightning shot from the gun and smashed into Cutter's back, sending the kid sprawling forward.

The blast smacked into John Henry, sending him over backward. He landed hard on the concrete, his head banging into the rough pavement. It felt as if he'd been hit by an eighteen-wheeler. And he hadn't taken the full impact of the shot. The kid had.

The blackness swirled around the edges of his vision, but he forced himself to hang on.

The gun was yanked out of his hand. There was nothing he could do to stop it.

"Grab Cutter," one voice said.

"Cops," another said. "We gotta get up outta here."

John Henry could hear the sounds of steps running off down the alley.

His mind said he had to follow them.

Had to get the gun.

Had to find out where it came from.

But his body wouldn't let him move as the blackness swept in over his eyes and took him.

CHAPTER 17

JOHN HENRY SAT IN ONE OF THE CURTAINED-OFF areas of the emergency room. The doctor had said he'd be all right in a few days and the headache would pass completely in a week. The doctor also said he was lucky.

John Henry didn't feel lucky at that moment. Norma had been admitted to the hospital earlier and was alive, but pretty beat up.

The police had come in and asked him hundreds of questions. He had done his best through his headache to answer, then he let the police lecture him about not chasing after a dangerous bank robber. It flowed over him like water and he responded with a series of nods. They had no way of knowing that he wasn't really trying to stop a bank robber.

He'd been after the weapon.

After three hours the doctor figured he wasn't going to go into shock or have convulsions from the knock on the head, so John Henry was released.

Martin and Grandma Odessa met him in the waiting room and helped him to the car.

After a good dinner and some of Grandma Odessa's special healing tea, he felt better. The headache had retreated to the level of a dull roar.

But he was just as angry.

Angry at himself for ever working on the weapons that could hurt his friends.

And angrier still at whoever let those weapons out onto the streets.

The next afternoon he found a pay phone a dozen blocks from Grandma Odessa's house. It was tucked against a wall where not much foot traffic passed and there was little street noise.

The call he placed was person to person to Colonel David. It took less than a minute to go through.

He told the colonel what had happened and exactly what he'd seen, including how the robbers had used the weapons to knock down a bank wall and blow up a police car.

"What'd you tell the police?" Colonel David said after he finished.

"What *could* I say?" John Henry shouted back at the colonel. "I *know* those damn weapons are top secret. I just wanna know how they hit the streets. That's all."

"Give me the pay-phone number you're at," Colonel David said, "and I'll call you back in ten minutes. I'll see if I can find out the answer to that question."

John Henry gave him the number and hung up. Then he slouched back against the wall, letting the heat of the afternoon ease his headache.

Down the block a bunch of grade-school-aged kids were playing, their laughing and yelling echoing up the street. If he didn't get these weapons off the street, there'd be no telling what sort of city those kids would grow up in.

Or if in ten years there would even be a city left standing.

For ten minutes he let the resolve sink in through the pain. Somehow, some way, he'd get those weapons and destroy them. Every last one of them.

The phone rang exactly one minute after Colonel David said it would.

Without so much as even a hello, Colonel David said, "NSA says every weapon created by us or by our civilian suppliers is accounted for."

"Colonel," John Henry said. "I know what I saw."

"You were upset, John," Colonel David said, his voice taking on an unnaturally soft edge. "You had just seen a friend get badly hurt and—"

"I had the weapon in my *hand*, sir," John Henry said, managing to keep his voice just below shouting level. "What do you think blew over that squad car? A twister? I caught a street-gang kid holding a USR Model 3.5 Sonic—"

"John, John," Colonel David said, quickly interrupting. "The phone you're using isn't secure."

"What the hell difference does that make, sir?" John Henry shouted. "We got to do somethin' about those weapons."

"Just *calm down*, mister!" the colonel shouted right back. "The NSA is on it. There's no way that highly classified weapons have ended up in the hands of some street gang. I just can't see how that's possible."

"I honestly don't know how you can see anything, sir," John Henry said, his voice shaking with anger. "With your head up your *ass*! Sir!"

He slammed the phone back into its cradle. The entire phone pulled from the wall and smashed to the sidewalk in a loud explosion of sound.

John Henry didn't care.

There was no help coming from the colonel, that much was clear. So he'd find the guns himself.

Ten minutes later, his anger just barely holding below the surface, he faced Martin in the kid's clutter-filled room.

"Who were they?"

Martin shrugged, but said nothing. He could obviously tell John Henry was mad.

John Henry refused to let it drop. "He had on a purple bandanna. You know who they are. I can tell."

Martin's face paled a little. "He was sportin' purple?"

John Henry only nodded, keeping his gaze boring through the kid. Finally he stepped back and took a deep breath. Martin wasn't at fault here. But he needed the kid's help.

"What's up, man?" John Henry said, making his voice as calm as he could considering how angry he was and how much his head hurt at that moment. "This isn't a joke. Who're you protecting and why, after what they did to Norma?"

"*You*, dammit!" Martin shouted, surprising John Henry with the force of the his response. "Purple is the Marks. Those kids are buckwild. They're the thickest gang out here."

John Henry moved close to Martin. "Where the hell are they? *Now!*"

Martin swallowed. "Back room at Benny's is where they usually hang."

John Henry nodded and turned around. "Believe me," he said, more to himself than Martin. "They're gonna hang."

CHAPTER 18

THE SMOKE SEEMED TO FILL EVERY INCH OF THE POOL hall and so many cigarette butts covered the dirty tile floor that the tiles were almost invisible. Well-worn booths filled one wall, the tables scarred and rough with hundreds of knife carvings. The peeling wallpaper had been ripped and covered with spray-painted slogans on every free inch. Most of them purple.

The old green felt of the three pool tables was ripped in a number of places and dotted with brown cigarette burns. The coin boxes of all three tables had long ago been ripped out. Only a few pool cues dotted the area and the cue ball on one table was so dirty it looked more like an eight ball.

John Henry stood in the door and glanced around. More than a dozen kids, all sporting purple clothing of some sort or another, were scattered around the room, slouching in chairs or sitting on the pool tables. Six of them were girls.

What flesh was showing on most of the kids had been tattooed. Two of the girls had nose and eyebrow rings.

Most of the guys wore muscle shirts, or ripped purple T-shirts.

Against the far wall a black-and-white television blared out a news report.

"As yet the police have no clues as to the perpetrators of this amazing, high-tech robbery, which has received worldwide attention. Over half a million dollars was stolen. In other news, the Los Angeles Lakers—"

One of the kids flicked off the television and turned to face John Henry as the room grew silent.

"Yo, dawg!" one said from near the first pool table. "Check out the Jolly Black Giant."

The others laughed.

John Henry strode directly into the middle of the room, heading for the kid who had spoken. He knew enough about gangs to know that usually only the leaders were allowed to speak up in situations like this one.

The members of the gang moved slowly around him into positions so that he was surrounded, like a pack of wild dogs around a lamb. But he had a sneaking hunch they'd soon discover he was no lamb.

John Henry stopped near one of the pool tables, facing the kid who talked. He was a short but well-muscled kid, with tattoos filling up the skin on both his arms and neck above his ratty T-shirt. He leaned against the other side of the table, smiling as if he didn't have a care in the world.

"Those guns you had," John Henry said over the table. "Where'd they come from?"

The kid laughed. "What are you talking about, man?"

"You know what I'm talking about," John Henry said, keeping his voice cold and calm and mean. "I just want to know where you and your boys got the weapons."

"Hey," the kid said, glancing around at the others

and laughing. "I'd like to know that, too. That heater was phat. Like to get me one."

"I hear that," another, larger kid said from the same side of the pool table that John Henry stood on.

John Henry glanced at the big kid who had just spoken, then back at the first one. It was clear they didn't have the weapons anymore, which was one good point. But where they got them was far more important.

"I thought you were the man," John Henry said. "I see you're just fronting."

"Hey, big boy," the first kid said. "What you see is what you get. You see him?"

The kid pointed at a big kid facing John Henry. The kid just smiled and his muscles rippled under his shirt, his tattoos moving like they had a life of their own.

"Now," the leader said, "you better raise up, fool, or the next time you go down you might not get back up."

So he'd been right after all. One of their gang members had been there in the alley when he got knocked down. But the kid he'd chased wasn't anywhere in sight. Most likely he'd never be in sight again if he had crossed this bunch.

"Where did you get those weapons?" John Henry repeated as low and as mean as he could, staring at the leader.

"Ohh," the muscled kid facing John Henry said, "look at me, shaking like a leaf."

Around the room others laughed.

Beside him two kids stepped toward John Henry, switchblades clicking open as they moved.

He took one out with a swift karate kick to the stomach, then the second with a fist to the side of the head.

Then with a spinning move he was on the muscled kid faster than the kid had time to react.

He grabbed him and lifted him off the floor, holding him in a painful grip that didn't allow the kid to move at all. A very useful grip he'd learned in the service, along with a hundred other useful things.

"Tell me what I want to know!" John Henry said to the kid, directly into his face, low and mean.

Around him the gang reacted. A dozen guns and knives were at his head, back, and throat.

Unfazed, he glared at the kid he held in the air. The kid was clearly in pain and not able to talk if he wanted.

"We don't play that shit," the kid in charge said from the other side of the pool table. His voice was slow and very mean. "We *know* you, Big Boy. So don't come around here no more."

John Henry instantly got the kid's message. He wasn't going to tell, ever. And he knew Martin and Grandma Odessa, and where they lived.

And he would think nothing of killing them.

John Henry glared at the kid he held in the air for one moment longer, then dropped him to the floor. The two he'd downed first still hadn't climbed back to their feet.

With a quick motion that scattered the gang members around him, he turned and headed for the door. About halfway there he stopped and looked back around. "You're gonna know me," he said, his voice clear and very angry. "A lot better."

CHAPTER 19

THE SMELL WAS ALWAYS THE FIRST THING TO GREET a visitor to the junkyard. A rotted-leather kind of smell that wasn't really offensive, just sort of "there." And much more "there" in the heat of a hot summer afternoon.

John Henry eased through the chainlike fence gate, closing it behind him, and was greeted immediately by Lillie, a beautiful golden retriever with a bushy tail that never seemed to stop wagging.

"Where's Uncle Joe?" he asked the dog.

She brushed against his leg and then spun around again, her tail going back and forth like it was her power source.

"All right, all right," he said and kneeled. "Petting first, Uncle Joe second." He scratched her ears for a good half minute, then stood and headed on into the junkyard, Lillie walking along beside him like she owned him and everything around them.

The pop of an acetylene torch being lit echoed through the junkyard. Then the rushing sound of the flame being turned up let John Henry know exactly where Uncle Joe was. He was in his "studio," as he laughingly called it.

Actually his studio was nothing more than a fairly empty area in the middle of twenty-foot-tall piles of junk.

John Henry, with Lillie at his side, moved into the studio area. There Uncle Joe cut with a torch at a large piece of metal that had been part of a refrigerator at one time in the distant past. Behind him, on a wooden platform, was a mass of metal he was shaping and building.

Uncle Joe's creations were strange-looking sculptures fashioned together from the odds and ends found in the yard. After retiring from the steel mill, he'd bought the old junkyard and started tinkering around with his strange form of art. Some of the local galleries had taken a few pieces and his work had caught on. Now there was no telling where his art ended up. Or the prices they brought.

Uncle Joe and John Henry had been friends since John Henry was a kid. There had been a number of times over the years when Uncle Joe had helped him with decisions. And today John Henry hoped the gray-haired old man would do so again. Only what troubled John Henry today wasn't so much a decision, as being lost. And in the past, when he was lost, he'd gone to Uncle Joe.

Uncle Joe greeted him with a wave and snapped off the torch. Suddenly the sounds of the city came back to the junkyard, as if the roar of the torch had kept them out.

"So where's this one going?" John Henry asked, walking a full circle around the strange mix of parts and metal Uncle Joe had on the wooden platform.

Uncle Joe laughed, wiping his hands on his sides. "To the Walker Museum in Minneapolis. They gave me a commission. Can you imagine?"

"Commission?" John Henry asked, smiling at the old man's wrinkled face and sheepish grin.

"Hey, if they want to say it's art, I ain't gonna try to talk 'em out of it."

"Don't blame you there," John Henry said.

Uncle Joe stared at his creation. "Sure pays good. I made ten times more since I retired than I did in thirty years at the steel mill."

"Well," John Henry said, moving around the sculpture. "I like it." And he did. He couldn't tell what it was supposed to be, but he liked it anyhow.

Uncle Joe stared at John Henry for a moment, then turned and went over to a cooler on the ground. He dropped down into a lawn chair and popped the lid on the cooler, rummaging around in the ice and water until he pulled out a can of root beer.

"Sit," he said, and motioned for John Henry to take the chair on the other side of the cooler. "Root beer?"

"Sounds good," John Henry said and took the offered cold can as he eased down into the rickety old lawn chair, hoping it still had enough strength to hold his bulk.

"So," Uncle Joe said after a long drink and an even longer sigh of relief. "Tell me about it."

John Henry glanced at his old friend. "That obvious, huh?"

Uncle Joe laughed, but said nothing.

Ten minutes later he finished telling Uncle Joe about what happened with Sparky, and with Norma and his visit to the gang pool hall.

Uncle Joe sat and listened, sipping his root beer and nodding. Finally, after John Henry had finished, the old man looked over at him. "So besides getting the weapons off the street, what else is on your mind?"

At first John Henry wanted to shout at his friend, *What else is there?* But then it hit him.

"I'm feelin' . . . like . . ."

Uncle Joe stared right into John Henry's eyes, clearly knowing what he was going to say, but not helping in the slightest.

"I feel responsible."

"How come?" Uncle Joe asked, not letting John Henry go from his gaze.

"Because I helped *create* 'em."

Uncle Joe nodded, downed a long gulp of root beer, and got to his feet, leaving John Henry sagging in the lawn chair. The old guy moved once around his sculpture, then started fiddling with the chunk he'd been cutting at.

"What you know about ol' Al Nobel?" he asked after a long minute.

"You mean like the Nobel peace prizes?" John Henry said. He was getting annoyed and he wasn't sure exactly why. "What difference does—"

"You know where that there prize money comes from?" Uncle Joe asked.

John Henry sure didn't much care at that moment, so he said nothing, just downed his root beer.

But Uncle Joe pushed on, ignoring John Henry's anger. "Ol' Al come up with somethin' he thought was gonna be great for mankind. Called it tri-nitro-tol-u-ene. TNT."

Somewhere, a long time ago, John Henry had learned that fact, but never put it together before.

"Ol' Al spent the rest of his life regretting his discovery."

"Feeling responsible," John Henry said softly.

"Exactly," Uncle Joe said, moving around and picking up his torch again as he studied the hunk he'd been cutting on.

"Responsible for all the people that died 'cause of it," Uncle Joe said. "So Al established prizes. For folks who work their asses off to make the world better."

John Henry rose out of his chair. He couldn't sit anymore. So he paced around Uncle Joe's sculpture, avoiding Lillie and the piles of junk that seemed to want to topple into the open area at any moment.

"What're you trying to tell me?"

Uncle Joe glanced up at John Henry. "I ain't trying to tell you nothing. Just saying everybody oughta do their best. If working in a metal shop's the best a man can do, then he needs to do it well."

Uncle Joe reached over and yanked on a chunk of the old refrigerator, but it didn't come loose. Then he went on. "Of course, if a man got skills for a higher calling, he damn sure better stretch out and use 'em."

John Henry snorted. "What kind of 'skills' are you talking about? I'd have to be made of this"—he pounded his fist on the top of a steel panel next to one pile of junk—"to take on all the new firepower out on the street. Even the police don't have a chance."

"Maybe the police ain't enough," Uncle Joe said, not looking at John Henry. "Maybe we need some new kind of firepower ourselves."

John Henry shook his head, starting to understand where Uncle Joe was heading, and not much liking it. He paced back and forth, two quick steps in one direction, then two back.

"Look, Uncle Joe," John Henry said. "I told myself when I left the service, I was done with those weapons. And even if I had some, they're top secret. We'd get busted before we got started."

Uncle Joe laughed. "We?" He shook his head and

went back to studying the old refrigerator, measuring it
for who knew what. "You speaking French now? And
besides, they can only get you if they know who you
are."

John Henry sighed. What Uncle Joe was saying made
sense. It was a way of fighting back. But he didn't see
how it would work. "My specialty isn't electronics, Uncle Joe. I worked strictly with metal. I couldn't build
one of those guns even if I wanted."

Uncle Joe nodded. "Yeah, I been meaning to ask you.
If I was gonna make me one of those—what do you call
'em—alloys? Y'know, to make metal stronger, exactly
what do I do?"

John Henry glanced at Uncle Joe, annoyed at the
seemingly stupid question right when they were talking
about something really important. "You add something
to it," he said. "You gotta add another element."

Uncle Joe smiled. "Oh, is that what you do?"

Suddenly John Henry understood. He glanced up into
the smiling face and bright eyes of Uncle Joe. Then he
laughed, went back over and sat down in the old lawn
chair.

"I got you, Uncle Joe," John Henry said. "I see what
time it is."

Uncle Joe smiled, reached over and with a pop lit his
acetylene torch. The blue-white flame cut through the
air, the solid base roar of the gas blocked out the sounds
of the city.

John Henry picked a fresh can of soda out of the ice
and cold water in the cooler, then let the sun warm his
skin as he sat and watched Uncle Joe cut an object apart
to create something new.

CHAPTER 20

THE OLD VA HOSPITAL SMELLED VERY MUCH LIKE A nursing home: antiseptic covering death. One smell layered in over the other for years and years, so thick it choked everyone who walked through the door. And John Henry was no exception.

The old hospital's tile floors and cracked plaster walls had long ago given up the fight of looking clean. The faded diamond pattern on the tile floor had worn completely off in two long, traffic-pattern lines, like lanes of a freeway viewed from the air. The maple wood trim around the doors and floor was scarred by a thousand bumps over the sixty years the place had existed. Even the very design of the place made it feel old and out of date: high ceilings and small, narrow doors with transoms. Huge round white lights hung from metal rods from the ceiling at even spaces down the halls. Only about half the lights worked.

The smell bit into John Henry's nose and made his stomach twist. He couldn't believe that Sparks had been in this place over the last few months. She deserved so much better. And he was going to make sure she got it.

He moved into the recreation room. An old box television was on in one corner, tuned to a soap opera. A
one-armed vet played Ping-Pong with another man in a
white cloth uniform, obviously one of the orderlies.

Sparks was sitting by herself on the far side of the
room. She faced a smudged window that looked out over
the lawn and trees around the back side of the building.

"Man, I thought my tax dollars went to keep these
windows clean," John Henry said.

No response at all from her. She just kept staring out
the window.

"How you doin', Sparky?"

He stuck out his finger, pointing it at her, waiting for
their ritual greeting.

Again she didn't answer or move. She looked like a
zombie, dressed in a white robe with food stains down
the front. Her cheeks were sunken, her hair looked dirty
and unkempt. It was clear to John Henry that his friend's
fire was almost gone. Where once had been bright eyes
and a smile there was a tight, dark mask of bitterness
and self-pity.

He kneeled down beside her. "Why'd you stop writing me back?" he asked. "Didn't you get my letters?"

She turned slowly and looked at him. "I got them,"
she said, her voice low and without energy. "And this
wheelchair you ordered. Thanks."

She went to turn to look back out the window, but he
grabbed the arm of her chair and spun her to face him.

"This all must be hard on you," he said, looking into
her sunken eyes. "I can imagine how you feel."

She half snorted at him. "I don't think so."

John Henry nodded. "You're right," he said. "I
don't. And I wish I could turn the clock back."

"Sometimes you don't get the choice," Sparks said. "Shit happens."

"Yeah," John Henry said, sitting back away from her. "I know. A good cop friend of mine just got hurt bad. With *one* of our weapons."

He took a deep breath and then went on. "Sparky, they're in the streets. The guns we built are in the hands of kids."

It seemed to take a moment for what John Henry said to get through the shell she'd put up around her, but then it did. And for the first time since he'd got there a spark of light returned to her eyes.

She looked up at him, a puzzled frown on her face. "On the street?"

He nodded.

"But how's that possible?"

"That's what I'm trying to find out," he said. "I could sure use your help."

Sparks patted her useless legs. "Yeah, right. I'd be a big help on the streets."

"What are you going to do?" John Henry said. "Just sit here and stare out that dirty window forever?"

Sparks's jaw jerked as if he'd slapped her. She turned away.

He could tell he'd hit her hard with that comment, but sometimes it took a good solid punch to get someone's attention. Right now his best friend needed help, and he was going to give it to her, even if she hadn't asked for it.

He stood, moved over to the old window. It had been painted shut years before. He took a good, long grasp on the sill and then shoved.

With a tearing sound the window smashed upward, rattling in its old frame.

He stepped back as a warm breeze blew Sparks' hair

back off her face. She stared out the open window and tears dripped down her cheeks.

"I . . . can't," she said slowly, not looking away from the window and the fresh air beyond. "You know the truth, Johnny? I just wanta die."

Now the tears were really flowing.

John Henry took a deep breath of the fresh air pushing back the smell of death and age in the old building. "You're talking crazy. Let's get out of here."

He moved around behind her and started to push her wheelchair toward the door.

"What are you doing?" she demanded. "No!" With a quick motion she clamped on the chair's brakes.

John Henry just laughed. "You think that's gonna stop me, you forgot who I am."

He reached down and picked her up, chair and all, as effortlessly as if he were carrying a baby's car seat.

"Irons!" she shouted. "Stop it! I don't wanna go."

John Henry laughed again. "Sorry, Sparks, sometimes you don't get a choice about things. This here's a prime example of shit happening."

He carried her out the door of the rec room and down the hall as the vets in the big room cheered and clapped.

CHAPTER 21

SPARKS DIDN'T SAY A WORD THE ENTIRE FLIGHT from St. Louis to Los Angeles, but John Henry didn't mind. He knew she'd come around. She had to. She was the only chance he had of stopping those weapons from filling the streets. And she had nothing to go back to except a long slow death.

After an hour's drive from the airport, he unloaded her from Uncle Joe's junk van and placed her easily into her chair, then wheeled her toward the gate of the junkyard. The day was one of those Southern California hot ones, with the smog holding in low over the valleys.

Sparks took a look at the piles of junk inside the fence and laughed. "I thought the hospital was funky. Who lived here before you, the Sanfords?"

He ignored her and opened the gate.

"Is it always this hot here?" she asked, fanning herself with her hand.

"Nope," John Henry said. "Sometimes it gets hotter."

"Oh, just wonderful," she said.

Uncle Joe's big golden retriever bounded around a pile of junk, wagging her tail. She ran right up to Sparks as if she'd known her for years.

Sparks smiled and petted her.

"That's Lillie," John Henry said as he closed the gate behind them. "She doesn't bite."

"Not your average junkyard dog," Sparks said.

"This isn't your average junkyard," John Henry said, and Sparks glanced up at him.

He pushed Sparks on into the yard, her chair bumping slightly over the rough surface, but not enough to make her uncomfortable. They rounded a large pile and Sparks said, "Amazing."

John Henry followed her look. She was staring at some of Uncle Joe's sculptures. He had half a dozen of them lined up along this area and they always awed anyone who came in.

Tucked behind the sculptures and off to one side between two piles of junk was a homegrown geodesic dome. John Henry had spent a full week shaping it from scrap. It looked odd from the outside, but John Henry knew it was solid, both earthquake-and waterproof.

"What's that?" Sparks asked, pointing at the dome.

"Just call it a little work in progress," he said.

She glanced around at him, then faced forward again as he wheeled her inside the dome.

The insides were ramshackle, but very clean and very neat. A dozen odd-shaped tables framed the sides of the room and formed a center island. On the tables was an assortment of lights, magnifiers, and tools.

An almost fully stocked workshop.

John Henry left her sitting in the middle of the concrete floor, staring around at the room. He went and opened a side door.

"Take a look at this," he said. "A full-sized bathroom, more than big enough for that chair of yours.''

"Very thoughtful," she said.

John Henry closed the door. "We fixed up another one for you at Uncle Joe's place. He's got a spare room all ready and—"

"Johnny," she said, turning her chair to face him directly. "What exactly am I supposed to be doing here?"

"Everything you did in the Army," he said. "We need to make our own counterweapons to take out the ones on the street. Fight fire with fire, so to speak."

She shook her head. "Man, are you crazy? We don't have the Army's resources."

"But we've got something they don't."

He pointed his long finger at her.

She only frowned and refused to complete their old ritual.

"Oh," John Henry said, looking down at his finger with a frown. "You're going to leave me hanging."

She shook her head in anger. "We need a lot more than just a cripple like me."

"Then you start making a list, darling," Uncle Joe said from the doorway.

He was carrying a big box, and somehow he still managed to get the door closed behind him.

He nodded to Sparks. "Hi. I'm Uncle Joe. Folks call me Uncle Joe."

He turned and faced John Henry. "Don't just stand there, shorty. Take this box."

John Henry took the box and slid it on top of a counter near Sparks.

"One thing about running a junkyard," Uncle Joe said. "People bring you the damnedest shit." With a nod of his head, Uncle Joe indicated that John Henry should take the stuff out of the box.

John Henry opened the box, then smiled and reached

inside. After a short tussle, he pulled out a computer and slid it on top of the counter.

"I can't believe it," Sparks said, rolling over and staring at the computer. "That's a mainframe IBM."

"IBM, A,B,C," he said. "Easy as one, two, three. Something like that." He laughed at his own joke.

Sparks just sat staring at the computer. "Where could you have possibly gotten—"

"Fella told me it fell off a truck," Uncle Joe said. He made a show of looking it over. "But it doesn't look too dented. If you knew how much stuff falls off trucks, you'd be in the junk game, too."

Sparks just glanced at Uncle Joe's smiling face. Then she nodded.

With a somewhat miffed look at John Henry, she said, "I'll make a list."

All John Henry could do was smile.

The light was back in her eyes.

They were a team again.

And that felt right.

CHAPTER 22

LAMONT LED MARTIN THROUGH THE FRONT DOOR OF Dantastic Productions and into the arcade showroom.

The afternoon was late, and only two customers stood near the blinking, brightly colored machines. Two salesmen in coats and ties talked near one desk and the receptionist looked bored behind the black marble counter. The room was about as quiet as it ever got during business hours.

"This place is a hit," Martin said, stopping and staring. "Man, I'm gonna own a spot like this one day."

Lamont stopped beside Martin. "That's why I'm trying to get you to put on."

Martin took a long look around the room. Then turned to Lamont. "So, what's up with this job? I'm trying to get paid."

Lamont waved away Martin's question. "The dude that own this shit is large. And I mean *large*. I want you to meet him."

From behind the two boys a voice echoed over the sounds of the machines. "Well, just call me Mr. Large."

Both boys spun around to see Burke stepping from the shadow of one of the pinball games. He stopped in front of them, looking Martin up and down.

Martin managed to keep himself from staring too long at the ugly red scar running the length of the guy's face. But it was a hard thing to do. He just didn't know where else to look.

"So, you must be Martin," Burke said. "I've heard a lot about you."

Then Burke turned to Lamont and with a clear force in his voice said, "I'll take over from here."

Lamont stepped back.

Burke draped his arm around Martin and expertly steered him toward the back of the arcade with only a glance back at the stunned look on Lamont's face.

Sparks struggled with the component rack, fighting to keep it on the table. In two days she had worked harder than she would have worked in a full week in the service. And even though she was tired, she felt better than she had since the accident.

A lot better, to be truthful.

Uncle Joe walked by, muttering to himself, her list in his hands. So far he'd managed to somehow create miracles. She wasn't sure how he did what he did, or where he got the money. And John Henry had warned her a few times to not ask. She had decided Johnny was right. She'd rather not know.

Last night during dinner Uncle Joe had asked her about her family. With her mother dead and her father in and out of alcoholic rehab, she told him she really didn't have a family.

He smiled and said, "Seems to me you do."

And then left it at that.

He was right and she knew it. Being here, with John

Henry, Uncle Joe, and Grandma Odessa felt like being with a family. And that was helping, too.

She twisted around in her chair, fighting the component rack into place. Then as she leaned back she brushed a screwdriver off the bench with her elbow.

The next moment was like a comedy of errors.

She reached to grab the tool, but her position in the chair caused her to slip forward.

Then she went to grab the arm of her chair, missed, and went forward even farther.

Somehow she managed to tuck her shoulder a little before she hit the floor, but the impact still half knocked the wind from her. Her wheelchair tipped over with a crash beside her.

"Shit! Shit! Shit!"

She could feel the tears filling her eyes. And the anger returning. The old anger from the VA Hospital.

She opened her mouth to call for help, then snapped it shut.

Behind her John Henry saw what happened and started toward her. Then he too stopped and said nothing, not even letting her know he was watching. Grandma Odessa had warned him that this moment would come. And she'd told him in no uncertain terms exactly what he was to do.

Nothing.

She lay there on the floor of the dome for a moment, forcing her anger back into place inside her. She couldn't always call for help. She was going to have to learn how to do this on her own someday.

Today seemed as good a day as any.

She took a deep, shuddering breath, wiped the tears from her eyes, and then scooted over beside her overturned wheelchair.

Bracing it against her useless legs, she flipped it back upright.

That was easier than she thought it would be. And with that thought she took another breath and went on.

She grabbed the fallen screwdriver, set the brakes on her wheelchair, and pulled herself up slowly.

Since losing her legs, her arms had gotten much stronger. But until she actually pulled herself off the floor and swung around in her chair she didn't know just how strong.

Back in place, she sat there breathing hard, letting the satisfaction fill her, reminding her of how it felt to be alive, to succeed.

It felt good. Damn good.

She brushed her hair back out of her eyes and looked up, right into the gaze of John Henry.

With only a nod to her, he turned and went back to work.

She sat staring at the sweat on his back for a moment as he moved back to the forge, then she smiled and also went back to work.

CHAPTER 23

THE HAMMER SMASHED DOWN OVER AND OVER, sending hot slivers of metal flying, as John Henry pounded on the thin plate of hot steel, forming it into the shape he wanted. The heat from the forge and the metal felt almost good against his skin. At times he wondered if he ever really felt at home unless he was working with steel. It was an odd love, but one he'd come to accept about himself.

"You work half the night here, don't you?" Sparks said.

He turned and smiled at her as she wheeled herself up next to him.

"You ever get tired?"

He nodded. "Yeah, I do. But then I think of who might get blasted by those weapons. What cop. What kid." He shrugged. "Makes me keep going."

He turned and pounded on the metal for another moment, then picked it up with the tongs and studied it. With a nod he set it down and turned to Sparks. "How are you doing? Got everything you need?"

"Yeah," she said.

Then she looked him directly in the eye and held the gaze for a moment. "Johnny," she said, her voice hesitant. "Thanks for everything. And for *not* helping me with everything. You understand?"

He smiled. "I understand." And he did understand. If he were in her spot he hoped others would do the same.

She pointed a finger at him.

With an even larger smile he reached out and touched the end of her finger with his.

That one touch felt great.

At that moment Martin bounced in the door, his energy breaking the moment between them. But John Henry knew that his friend Sparks was completely back. No matter what happened now, she'd make it.

"Yo, y'all," Martin said. "Grandma Odessa wants you to come check out her Cajun catfish stuffed with crawdaddy mousse and served à l'orange. Whatever that is."

Sparks shook her head and glanced at John Henry with a smile. "That is an amazing concept."

Martin moved over and looked down at the metal John Henry had been working on. "What are y'all making?"

John Henry wiped his hands off with a paper towel. "Just working on some gadgets."

"Top secret shit, huh?" Martin said.

"Yeah, actually it is," John Henry said. "Why do you have to curse all the time?"

John Henry took a playful jab at Martin, then wadded up the paper towel into a tight ball. With a quick toss he lobbed the towel at the wastebasket. And missed.

With a shrug he turned back to Sparks. "Y'all go ahead. I'll be up in a minute."

Sparks smiled at him, then swung her chair around.

"How's your new job?" she asked Martin as they moved toward the door.

"It's dope," Martin said, the excitement clear in his voice. "The boss made me his main man. Said if I studied up, I could make mad cream. Be mad powerful."

Sparks shrugged. "If that's what you're in it for."

Martin laughed. "Yo, C-R-E-A-M," he said, spelling out the word. "Cash Rules Everything Around Me. Cream. Get it? Get the money, dollar, dollar, bill, y'all."

John Henry laughed and Sparks glanced back at him, a puzzled look on her face. It was clear to John Henry that she was having problems following Martin. To be honest, he had the same problem once in a while.

Then, as they went through the door she said to Martin, "Some things money can't buy."

"What it can't get, I can't use," he said, shaking his head in disgust. "You'd blow up at my job."

Again John Henry just laughed and then turned and went back to pounding on steel.

After they were outside, Martin turned and looked directly at Sparks. "John Henry says you're a genius."

Sparks laughed, but inside she felt really good. Being back with John Henry made her feel whole. And his high opinion of her made her feel even better.

"John Henry exaggerates," she said to Martin.

"Not likely," Martin said, laughing, as they headed for Grandma Odessa's.

CHAPTER 24

THE NEXT WEEK WENT QUICKLY.

John Henry stayed at the forge seemingly day and night.

Uncle Joe kept working on the dome and the lab, bringing Sparks the parts she needed.

Sparks stayed at the computer and the workbenches, half the time staring at a three-dimensional image of a schematic on the screen, the other half wearing surgical magnifiers over her eyes while she worked on half a dozen small electronic devices.

Then finally they were almost ready.

She wheeled her chair out near John Henry's forge as he worked with a thin piece of curved metal against his upper leg. She motioned for him to come over and he followed her request.

"Okay, big guy," she said. "Tonight's the night. You about ready?"

"Almost," he said.

She turned her chair around and wheeled herself back inside the dome while he followed. The dome, over the short time she'd been here, had grown into a state-of-the-art electronics lab, though not at all like the Army would have done it. This lab was full of charmingly homey and piecemeal equipment that worked together like fingers in a glove.

She moved over to the counter, picked up a small piece of plastic, and grinned at him.

"Stick it in your ear."

"Funny," he said. Then with a quick, curious glance at the small piece of plastic, he did as she instructed.

She slipped on a phone headset and turned away from him.

"Do you read?" she asked.

Her voice came clear and sharp through his ear. "Five by five," he said. "Receiver only?"

"Nope," she said. "Transceiver. So watch what you say about me. Good for about thirty miles. So's this."

She handed him a button-sized camera with a small battery pack. Then she turned and pointed to one of the monitors on her bench. It displayed a fish-eyed image of John Henry's face as he stared into the tiny camera.

"Great," he said. For some reason knowing that Sparks was with him while he was on the streets instantly made him feel better. Safer.

He glanced up at Uncle Joe as the older man entered the dome carrying a large stainless-steel sledgehammer.

"Yo," John Henry said, pointing at the hammer. "What's that?"

Uncle Joe handed the hammer to John Henry, then stepped back smiling.

"Man named John Henry has to have a hammer," Sparks said. " 'Course I designed it to do more than pound things."

"My favorite part is the *shaft*," Uncle Joe said.

Both John Henry and Sparks gave Uncle Joe a "I can't believe you said that" look.

"What?" Uncle Joe said, pretending to be puzzled.

Sparks spent the next twenty minutes explaining every feature of the hammer. And it had a lot of them, from a deployable long-range communications array to a sonic rifle with hidden scope. It could also take a pounding just like a regular sledgehammer.

When Sparks had finished, John Henry dropped down into a chair. "I appreciate what you two have done, but I gotta handle this alone. It might get ugly."

Sparks laughed. "I'm used to ugly. I've been dealing with you, right?"

"I'm serious," he said. "It could get dangerous."

"Hey," Uncle Joe said. "I boogie around danger like a *Soul Train* dancer." Then he turned very serious. "You do what you started out to do, son. We're with you."

He nodded.

"So," Sparks said, "I'm ready for a little field test."

John Henry nodded. "I need to just finish the one last piece."

"Then go to it, big boy," Sparks said.

One hour later outside at the forge, Uncle Joe watched as John Henry finished the last piece, the molten metal glowing red hot as he pulled it from the fire.

"I know you wanted to stay away from the weapons work, son," Uncle Joe said. "But—"

John Henry stopped him. "Sometimes, you gotta fight fire with fire."

Sparks wheeled up behind them.

"Sometimes," she said, "we use what we are given to fight the fights we can fight." She looked at John Henry. "This is your fight. You know that."

He nodded, then turned and drew a hunk of metal from the forge.

"Wow," Uncle Joe said.

"You can say that again," Sparks said.

Slowly John Henry held up the fearsome-looking mask of glowing steel. Part mask, mostly helmet, it would conceal his face and hair and protect his head.

John Henry examined it carefully, then plunged it into a tub of water. With a hiss the helmet disappeared. A few moments later John Henry pulled out the gleaming mask.

"I'll be damned," Uncle Joe said softly. "John Henry Irons has turned himself into the man of *steel*."

CHAPTER 25

THE HEAT OF THE DAY STILL LINGERED INTO THE early evening. The concrete of the sidewalk radiated a warmth that in the winter would have felt good, but on this evening only made the air more humid and sticky.

Dorie Kearny and Jon Merchant walked arm in arm, enjoying the summer evening and each other's company. They were both dressed casually for the heat and both had the money to make even casual look good. They'd been dating now for almost four months and with each time it just got better and better. Tonight had been dinner and a movie. A block walk to his BMW and then back to her house in the hills for the night.

Suddenly the perfect date turned into a nightmare.

Out from behind a parked car a man came at them. He wore the clothes of a street person, ragged, dirty, and layered, even in the heat. A white man, he wore a black stocking cap and had a beard that was dirty and tobacco-stained.

Jon noticed him first, but by then it was too late. The

mugger flashed a knife and shoved Jon against the building wall, banging his head in the process.

"What—" Dorie tried to say before she too was slammed against the wall beside Jon.

The mugger waved the knife in front of both of them. "Don't give me no *shit*!"

"All right," Jon said, holding up his hands. "Just take it easy now."

The mugger laughed at him, his rancid breath washing over both of them with a smell they would not soon forget. "You lemme see some cash."

He flashed the knife in front of Jon's face, then moved slowly to Dorie. "Break yourself," he said, smiling at Jon. "Now!"

Dorie raised her purse for the guy to take. "Here. Just don't hurt us."

Jon held his wallet between his fingers and handed it to the mugger.

"On the ground," the mugger said.

Then as Jon and Dorie complied he turned and ran down the street and to the right into an alley behind a liquor store.

"Thank god," Dorie said and burst into tears.

Jon reached out and the two sat on the sidewalk holding each other, both shaking.

The mugger moved quickly down into the alley and over to a closed dumpster. There he emptied the purse onto the top of the metal, scattering aside a few family photos Dorie had brought to show Jon later in the evening.

"That any way to treat somebody's family pictures?" a deep voice said from the shadows.

The mugger snapped around, the knife in his hand. But he didn't see anyone.

"Who's zat!" the mugger shouted. "I'll shank you, man! Don't mess with me."

The voice responded, "Just give 'em their money and belongings back and we won't have a problem."

The mugger faced the shadow, his knife held in front of him. "I ain't got no problem."

"Oh, yes you do," the voice said.

And then John Henry Irons stepped into the light facing the mugger.

Only now he was no longer identifiable as John Henry. He was completely wrapped in form-fitting, shining stainless steel. He was carrying a huge steel hammer slung over his shoulder. And at seven feet two inches of muscles and steel, he was a very imposing figure.

He was Steel.

The mugger's knife dropped to the ground and his eyes bugged out in total surprise.

John Henry smiled to himself at the mugger's reaction to his looks. It was exactly as he hoped it would be.

In John Henry's earpiece he heard Sparks's voice. "Surprise."

And behind her statement he could also hear Uncle Joe laughing at the mugger's face. They could both see everything around John Henry through the monitors built into his helmet. With four monitors and Sparks watching, it was as if Steel had eyes on every side of his head.

The mugger panicked and bolted toward the end of the alley and the street beyond. In two steps Steel grabbed him, lifted him off the ground, and slammed him into the wall.

Then putting his steel-masked face right into the mugger's, he said, "Hang around a minute."

Steel raised his other fist, aimed his wrist bracelet, and fired. A metal spike rammed through the mugger's dirty jacket and pinned the guy to the wall.

"Oh," Sparks said in John Henry's ear. "That works great."

John Henry had to agree. It had been Uncle Joe's idea to include the wrist-spike weapon. And already it had come in handy. Very handy.

The mugger grew even more terrified at the sound of the exploding spike. "Don't kill me!" he pleaded with Steel. "I got a wife and kids and—"

"Remember how this feels," Steel said, stepping back and letting the mugger hang on the wall from his coat. "Do it again and that's your ass."

The mugger nodded so hard he banged his head against the brick wall.

"I think that boy's been born again," Uncle Joe said in John Henry's ear.

A half block away, Jon and Dorie had found a pay phone and were frantically trying to call 911.

Then Jon slammed the phone back into the cradle. "Can you believe this shit?" he shouted. "911's busy! How can it be busy?"

Dorie glanced past him, then shook her head, her gaze clearly on something beyond Jon. Finally she patted Jon on the arm and without taking her gaze off what she was staring at, she got him to turn around.

Towering over them was Steel. He was holding out her purse and Jon's wallet.

"I think these belong to you."

Dorie nodded.

Jon reached out and took his wallet, then her purse from Steel. "Yes," he said at a glance at what he held. "They do. Thank you."

"Tell the police that your mugger is hanging on a wall just down that alley."

Jon nodded.

"And on behalf of the citizens of L.A., I'd like to apologize. Y'all be cool."

With that Steel turned and at a smooth run disappeared down the dark street.

CHAPTER 26

STEEL DUCKED DOWN AN ALLEY AND THEN INTO some shadows. He was breathing hard and excited. The first light test had worked. And the armor had gotten the reaction he had hoped from the mugger. But there was still a lot to test. There were bound to be some problems before the night was through.

"You see everything?" he asked softly, talking to Sparks and Uncle Joe after making sure no one was near.

"And taped it so you can watch the reruns," Sparks said. "Nice job."

"Thanks," John Henry said. "Everything reading out five by five?"

"Your body temp's up a little," Sparks said. "We gotta think a little more about ventilation."

"I'm fine," he said.

"The other readings are all on the mark."

John Henry knew that she was facing a bank of monitors and oscilloscopes. She had everything wired into those computers of hers, including his heartbeat. He felt very secure having her with him like that.

Uncle Joe's voice came in clear in John Henry's ear. "Police scanner just lit up. They talkin' about a gang bang heating up down off Hill Street."

"Let's not bite off more than we can chew," Sparks said. "Remember, we're on our first night out here."

"Give me a cross street," John Henry said.

And in his ear he heard Sparks sigh.

And that sigh made him smile.

The streetlights cast odd shadows through the palm trees of Pershing Square park. Paths had been worn through some of the grass by daytime pedestrians, and parked cars surrounded the small square of green like a fence. At night the park was never crossed. It was far too dangerous.

The sounds of the city and nearby freeway created a dull roar over the park like a blanket covering a bed, always there, and only noticed when not present. Suddenly sharp gunshots echoed off the nearby buildings and through the park, slicing through the background noise as if it didn't exist.

Three members of the Skins street gang sprinted into the park and headed diagonally across, their black bandannas flapping in the wind as they ran.

A low-rider car, its small tires screeching on the pavement, careened around the corner of the park and accelerated to cut off the three Skins members. A Hispanic kid, not more than eighteen, with a whispy-thin mustache, leaned out of the car, a pistol in his hands. He was waving the pistol around, and it was clear by how he held it he knew exactly how to use it.

The three Skins gang members reached the far edge of the park slightly ahead of the low-rider, cut between two cars and sprinted past a parked van, using the parked cars as shields.

As they ran past, John Henry stepped out into the street and faced the car, his hands on his hips. This fight was going to stop now.

The car screeched to a halt twenty feet from Steel.

After a moment the driver leaned out of the car, then looked over at the kid in the passenger seat with the gun. "Damn, homey!" he said, slapping his hand against the driver's door. "What the hell is *that*?"

The kid hanging out the passenger-side window shouted at Steel. "Move out th'way, fool. This is our hood."

Steel didn't move. But using the deepest, most powerful voice he could manage he said, "In my hood, they call me the benchwarmer." He knew that would get them wondering what he was talking about, and he was right.

The two in the car glanced at each other, then the one with the gun asked, "Benchwarmer?"

"Yeah," Steel said, " 'cause *I don't play*."

He took a deep breath and let his words echo off the buildings and parked cars. Then he said, "Put the gun down and there won't be trouble."

The gunman laughed. "Man, please," he said, shaking his head from side to side in amazement while he laughed. "I'm about to smoke you like a blunt."

He leveled the pistol right at Steel and fired.

John Henry made himself keep his eyes open as the bullets hit his armor. He could feel the impact of each, but not enough to make him even stagger. The armor held solid as six bullets hit and bounced.

In his ear he heard Uncle Joe say, "Do I want to look?"

Sparks's voice said, "One of us has to."

"I'm fine," he said to them without moving his lips

and only loud enough for Sparks and Uncle Joe to pick up.

For a moment the two in the car just stared, not really believing what they had just seen. The gunman even looked down at the empty pistol in his hand, then back at Steel, as if checking to see if he had actually fired.

"Enough of this shit!" the driver of the car said, ducking his head back inside the window and slamming the car into gear. "Let's get a body."

"Uh, Johnny—" Sparks's voice said in John Henry's ear.

He'd been carrying the hammer in a specially made sling on his back. With a quick movement he brought it over his arm and snuggled the hammer head against his shoulder like the butt of a rifle.

His steel-gloved hands held the shaft of the hammer in a natural firing position. He could feel a switch clearly under his left thumb.

"Sonic is forward?" he asked Sparks softly as the car gained speed toward him. "Right?"

"Yeah, yeah," Sparks said. *"Forward."*

"It's hammer time," John Henry said and pulled the trigger.

There was a solid *thump* as the hammer fired.

The onrushing car was met by a dusty shock wave of sound as hard as a brick wall and far, far more powerful.

The back end of the car snapped up into the air like a horse trying to buck off a rider.

The two inside went through the front windshield with an explosion of glass. They hit the pavement and bounced, tumbling to stop not more than ten feet in front of Steel.

"Well, I'll be dipped in shit and rolled in bread crumbs," Uncle Joe said.

"One of Grandma Odessa's recipes, no doubt," Sparks said.

Steel stepped forward and stood over the two boys, both of whom were slowly coming around. As one looked up at him, Steel said, "Should always buckle up."

"Behind you," Sparks said.

He turned just in time to see three more gang members step out into the streetlight, stop and raise their guns.

John Henry flipped a tiny red switch on his hammer, then held it tight against his armor.

"Electromagnet engaged," Sparks said. "Make sure your footing is solid."

John Henry spread his legs and braced himself as around him the oddest things started to happen. First the guns were snatched out of the gang members' hands. They flew through the air and smacked against John Henry's suit in a series of loud clangs.

Then knives from their pockets were in the air, followed by two hubcaps from a nearby parked car.

Metal-framed glasses, a watch, a trash-can lid, all flew at John Henry.

"What a magnetic personality," Sparks said.

The gang members stood amazed, staring at Steel.

Then as one they turned and ran like they'd seen a ghost. A steel ghost.

John Henry clicked off the magnetic field and all the guns and knives and odd items that were stuck to him dropped to the street in a loud metal-on-metal sound.

"Uncle Joe tells me," Sparks said, "that the police scanner says you're about to have official company."

"Understood," Steel said.

"And you've got two more misguided youths," Sparks said, "coming up on your back with baseball bats."

John Henry pivoted, swinging his hammer around. He caught one of the bats solidly, knocking it out of the kid's hands and clear over the fence of cars into the park.

Then with another quick move he knocked both gang members off their feet and onto their backs.

"Yo," one of them said, eyes wide, staring up at Steel. "You got eyes in the back of your head?"

"No doubt," John Henry said. "And I'll be watching you. Count on it."

They both stared at him, clearly getting his message.

He stood over them, holding the hammer like it might come down on them at any moment. "So clean up your act," he said. Then he stepped back. "Now, do like a rash and break out."

Without having to wait for a second chance, they both scrambled to their feet and headed off. The two who had gone through the car window were also limping off toward a nearby alley. Only Steel stood in the street now.

"Good work, Sparky," he said.

"Hey," Sparks said. "Be my leg man. I'll have eyes for you."

"Deal," he said as the sounds of police sirens filled the park area.

"You got more blue coming," Sparks said.

"Got them," John Henry said. "From the south and west." He could clearly see their lights flashing off the buildings as they screamed toward him.

"He knows a way outta this?" Uncle Joe said to Sparks, but John Henry clearly heard.

"Oh," Sparks said, "I'm sure he does."

John Henry just smiled to himself.

"Don't you, Johnny?" she said.

"I sure hope so," he said. And as the cop cars surrounded him, that hope grew much, much stronger.

CHAPTER 27

PETER TRIMBLE HAD BEEN A COP FOR EXACTLY SIX months and three days. And for most of that time he'd been riding with Jack LaSalle, a veteran of twenty-three years. He'd heard stories that he wouldn't have believed if Jack hadn't told them. Jack wasn't the type to ever hype anything beyond the truth. After being a cop in Los Angeles for that long, he just didn't have to. He'd seen it all.

Jack slid the black and white around the corner and to a stop in the middle of the street.

Directly in front of them was a sight that even Jack would never have imagined. A smashed gang car and a huge man dressed in steel armor of some kind. Around the man's feet were at least half a dozen odd guns and another eight knives, along with hubcaps and assorted other items.

"Would you look at that?" Jack said.

"Weird," was all Peter could say.

"This story is going to be a good one," Jack said, laughing to himself. "I can just tell."

Jack climbed out, gun drawn.

Peter did the same on the other side, both men keeping the door of the police car between them and the huge man in the middle of the street.

The giant guy had been holding a huge hammer and as they climbed out of the car he slipped it over his shoulder into a sling of some sort.

Jack grabbed the mike and flipped it for external. Then he said, ''Okay, Sir Lancelot. Step away from those weapons.''

The huge guy did as he was told, moving with a light step that Peter wouldn't have thought possible with that much steel on him. The stuff must only be a tinfoil costume of some sort. But it sure looked real enough.

''Get those hands up,'' Jack ordered. ''Way up.''

The steel man did as he was told, then Peter saw something shoot from the guy's wrist toward the top of a nearby building.

The man in armor grabbed one hand on the other wrist and just lifted off the ground, headed right at the top of the building, almost as if he were flying.

''I don't think you meant that high, did you, Jack?'' Peter said to his openmouthed partner.

''Nice shot,'' Sparks said into John Henry's ear as the spike from his wrist buried itself into the top edge of the roof of the three-story building, sending strong anchors into the masonry and brick. ''You been practicing?''

''Every night,'' John Henry said softly. ''Now let's just hope my arm doesn't come out of the socket.''

He punched a small key on his wrist. His wristband whirred to life, retracting the incredibly strong, incredibly thin steel wire hooked to his armor and the spike embedded in the top of that building.

With a yank, he was off the ground and moving to-

ward the top of the building. The retracting mechanism
had been built by Sparks to slow as it neared the end. It
worked perfectly, allowing him to slow his ascent and
grab the top ledge of the roof with one hand while re-
leasing the cable from the spike with the other.

He swung over onto the roof and looked back at the
street. He'd so surprised the cops they hadn't even had
time to get off a shot.

"The man of steel can fly," Uncle Joe said. "I am
simply amazed."

"Nice, huh?" Sparks said.

John Henry quickly ran to the far side of the building
and surveyed the distance between it and the next building. From below it hadn't looked anywhere near as far
across the gap as it did now, standing up here looking
down.

"Don't even think about it," Sparks said. "My computer says you can't make it."

"Piece o' cake, Sparky," John Henry said.

"No," she said, her voice in his ear insistent. "The
range finder says it's too far."

John Henry backed up ten steps. "Girl," he said. "In
high school I finished second in the long jump. You
didn't know?"

Now Sparks was shouting in his ear. "Don't put your
macho bullshit up against my computer. You weren't
wearing seventy-five pounds of—"

He started running at the edge.

"Johnny!" she shouted.

He leaped.

In his ear he heard Uncle Joe gasp.

Instantly he knew Sparks was right. He wasn't going
to make it.

With every ounce of strength, he had he managed to

grab onto the edge of the next building and hang on as his body smashed down into the wall.

Then, with his wind half knocked out of him, he pulled himself back up over the edge and stood.

Too close.

Way too close.

"Okay," he said, taking a deep breath and glancing back over the edge. "One for the computer."

"I guess that's why you came in second," Sparks said. "Now quit trying to breathe and get going. The cops are on the building you just left."

CHAPTER 28

JOHN HENRY MOVED QUICKLY TO THE FAR SIDE OF the second building and glanced down. He was right where he planned to be, three stories above the alley.

Quickly he fired another spike into the concrete ledge around the rooftop, set the wire release on his wrist, and stepped off the edge.

The jerk of the wire catching him yanked him against the brick building, but his armor took most of the shock and he kept descending.

"Thirty feet," Sparks said in his ear.

"Twenty."

"Ten."

He cut the wire loose when she said ten, but his timing was off. The sudden loss of the restraining wire from above flipped his feet up slightly.

He landed on his back in a pile of boxes and trash.

"Johnny?" Sparks asked, her voice climbing in intensity in his ear. "Johnny? You all right?"

He sat up, then shook his head. "Just a little trashed, that's all."

"Guess we better do a little work on the release timing on those landings," she said.

He stood and brushed off some sticky garbage from the metal plates on his legs. "That would be nice."

"Hey," Sparks said. "This is a work in progress. Uh-oh."

"Don't say 'uh-oh,' " Steel said. "Makes me jumpy."

"Sorry," Sparks said. "Only you're about to have company again."

"Got 'em," he said.

Quickly he ducked behind a dumpster and headed for a pile of boxes in an alcove off the alley. There, under the boxes, right where he left it, was his motorcycle.

But this motorcycle was like no other on the road. Fluidly designed, and made out of polished, lightweight steel, it looked fast just sitting still. It was longer and sleeker than a normal bike, and every part was fully formed and custom cast from stainless steel just like his armor.

When John Henry, in his Steel armor, leaned forward, low and tight over the bike, he became one with the bike, his armor blending and fitting with the motorcycle like the old hand-and-glove routine. The best blending of man and machine on any road.

And most likely the fastest.

He was also the most powerful, with an arrowlike sonic cannon mounted to the front. Not even a full tank could stand in the way of this bike if Steel didn't want it to.

John Henry swung onto the seat as if he were home. Just being aboard the bike gave him a feeling of safety. He clicked the engine to life and felt the powerful vibration through his armor.

"Ready," he said.

"Bring her home," Sparks said.

With a mighty roar, he smashed out into the open and right past the cop car at the end of the alley.

"Now that must have looked cool," Sparks said in his ear. "Too much fun."

Inside the cop car the young cop named Peter watched as Steel sped past. "Wow," he said. "Heavy."

Jack shot him a sharp look, then spun the car and headed in pursuit.

Peter grabbed the mike. "Suspect fleeing on a chopped silver motorcycle, heading east on Olive. We are in pursuit."

"He's heading right into traffic," Jack said. "See if you can get his plate."

Peter leaned forward, straining to see the shining silver letters on the plate on the back of the bike. Slowly he could make them out. "Sierra, Tango, Echo, Echo, Lima."

Peter laughed, then glanced at Jack as the older cop swung the car between two other cars and accelerated after the bike.

"Steel," Peter said, laughing. "Well, duh."

"You find this guy interesting, huh?" Jack said, braking to miss a stupid driver who didn't know enough to get out of the way for a police siren.

"Y'gotta admit," Peter said. "The guy's got style."

Jack snorted. "Style, my ass."

In front of them loomed the Los Angeles Music Center, as the traffic light on First and Olive went from green to yellow. The big guy on the bike barely made it through.

Ahead of Steel, the signal at Grand Avenue in front of the Dorothy Chandler Pavilion, turned red, and solid cross traffic filled the intersection.

"Sparky?" Steel said. "The light?"

"I see it," Sparks said. "Hang on."

"Uh-oh," Uncle Joe said.

"I don't want to hear no 'uh-oh,' " John Henry said.

"We're cool," Sparks said. "Just a little high-tech trouble, is all. Uncle Joe fixed it with a quick kick."

Ahead of Steel the lights at the intersection started flashing all colors. Red, green, yellow, then back to red.

"Nothing looks fixed to me," John Henry said.

"Hey," Sparks said. "It ain't easy being green."

There was a slight pause that seemed to last forever at John Henry's speed, then she said, "There."

The light at the intersection turned to solid green and stayed that way. The cross traffic suddenly hit their brakes and Steel did a few quick moves and was through.

"I'm getting too old for this shit," Uncle Joe said in John Henry's ear, obviously breathing hard.

"Now this should close the door," she said. "I'll turn the signal back to red behind you."

"Good thinking," John Henry said.

With a quick turn he whipped the bike around the corner onto Flower Street, passing the Bonaventure and cutting right onto the Seventh Street bridge over the Harbor Freeway.

Behind him two cop cars were now in the chase, but they were a distance back.

"I should be able to give you green all the way home," Sparks said.

"And red for them."

"Of course," she said, laughing.

In only a moment he was back in the old neighborhood. He cut a corner and headed onto Bixel Street. But where the gate should be was a tall wooden fence.

"Sparks?"

"No trust," she said.

At the exact right moment a hidden gate in the wooden fence snapped open and Steel flashed through.

"Welcome home," Sparks said.

Steel streaked through the junkyard as in the distance a helicopter's light filled the tops of the trees.

At full speed he headed for a huge pile of junk near one edge of the yard. Just at the last moment again a small section of the junk heap opened like a garage door.

Steel flashed inside and slid the bike to a stop while behind him the door snapped shut.

The first test was finished.

CHAPTER 29

STEEL STROLLED INTO UNCLE JOE'S GEODESIC DOME, smiling under his helmet. Both Uncle Joe and Sparks laughed and applauded as he entered.

"Man," Uncle Joe said. "I ain't felt this good since the Mets won the Series in '68."

John Henry pulled off his helmet and laughed. "The Mets won in '69, Uncle Joe."

"See," Uncle Joe said, moving to slap John Henry on the back, then thinking better of hitting the steel armor. "It's been a long time."

"Man," John Henry said, talking fast in his excitement, "when that wire pulled me up to the top of that building my heart stayed on the ground."

"When it released in the alley," Sparks said, "and you ended up on your back, my heart *stopped*."

"Work in progress, huh?" John Henry said and laughed. "Did you see the faces on those kids?"

"They acted like they found Jesus," Uncle Joe said.

"Uh, excuse me," Sparks said, pointing at John Henry. "Next time trust your range finder before you jump. Okay?"

"No argument," he said.

Uncle Joe moved around and started to help John Henry off with the armor. His skin underneath was bruised and soaked with sweat. But as the armor came off John Henry felt almost naked without it. Only one night out and he was already that used to wearing it.

"Ouch," Sparks said, pointing at the bruises. "Those must really hurt."

John Henry only shrugged. "Part of the job." He looked down, then shook his head. "Not even sure when or where I got them."

"Good thing this is stainless," Uncle Joe said, wiping the sweat off one part of the armor. "Otherwise you'd be rusting."

"True," John Henry said as the evening air drifted around him, cooling him. He wiped down his face and arms, then slipped on a shirt. "Lots of work to do. The bike felt a little rough toward the end. I think we need to give it a good tuning."

Sparks laughed. "You think you've got things to do— I've got a printout coming up so we can evaluate everything. You're not going back out there until we do."

John Henry smiled at her. "Sparky," he said, "don't know what I'd do without you."

He pointed a long finger at her and she lightly touched it with hers in their ritual greeting.

"Really?" she asked.

John Henry held her gaze. "No doubt."

"Thanks," she said softly. "You're all right yourself."

They let their gazes hold for a moment longer before Uncle Joe broke the spell by clearing his throat.

Both of them laughed, then John Henry turned. "C'mon, Uncle Joe," he said. "Let's take a look at that bike."

John Henry rolled up the wet towel he'd been using into a tight ball and lobbed it toward a laundry basket on the shelf.

And missed.

With a laugh he shrugged and headed for the secret garage. They all had work to do. The first test had been a success. But the real mission was yet to start.

CHAPTER 30

THE LIGHTS OF A DOZEN ARCADE GAMES FLASHED, not making much of an impact under the bright fluorescent lights of the workshop. Four technicians worked over two games while Martin stood to one side talking to them.

"Man, I tell you, he was jetting past us, doing like eighty."

"Right," one of the techs said, laughing. "A man covered in steel riding a motorcycle?"

Martin gave him his hardest stare.

Then a hand clamped down on his shoulder and he spun around into the scarred face of Burke.

"Morning, Martin," Burke said, smiling while the other techs scrambled to work even harder.

"What's up, Mr. Large," Martin said.

"I hear you've gotten interested in the new microchip game technology."

Martin shrugged. "Yeah, I think that new interactive unit sounds—"

"Fly?" Burke said, naming the game. "Let's you and me have a look."

With an arm firmly on Martin's shoulder, Burke led him away from the other techs. After a dozen steps he stopped.

"You really saw that man last night?" Burke asked.

"Covered in steel," Martin said. "Yeah, he was tight. Got him some skills. And a brother."

"Really?" Burke asked, glancing around to make sure no one could hear. "You think he was from your neighborhood?"

"Damn sure not from Beverly Hills," Martin said, laughing. "Damn sure."

"Tell me about your neighborhood," Burke said. "Where *exactly* do you live?"

The smells of Foster's Grocery always made Grandma Odessa smile. Fresh-baked bread greeted her like an old friend as she entered, followed by the smells of detergents along the left aisle. Then to the back for the crisp, dirt smell of fresh vegetables. The place was a smorgasbord of smells and she loved it.

As she lingered near the front counter in the fresh-baked bread smell, the television over the counter got turned up by Lenonard Foster, the owner. "Listen to this, will ya," he said, more to himself, she was sure, than to the customers waiting in the checkout line.

On the screen, a newscaster approached a well-dressed couple. It looked like this had been taped at night over by the park.

"So what did he look like?" the announcer asked the couple.

"About seven feet six," the man said. "Huge."

Beside him the woman nodded.

"Big as a mountain," the man went on. "And covered in stainless steel from head to foot."

"That's right," the woman said. "He caught the mugger and returned our money, you know. Plus my purse and his wallet. He was extremely polite.''

Mr. Foster left the sound up, but turned around to help the first in line, shaking his head as he did.

''Never heard anything like that,'' he said.

Neither had Grandma Odessa. But she had a sneaking hunch who might be involved. They had to be doing *something* over there at Uncle Joe's all the time.

The lake in Echo Park looked smooth, almost glassy, under the hot sun of the afternoon. It reflected the city skyline like a mirror and did nothing to cool down the area around it. Burke even wagered it heated up the park, what with all the light reflecting off the surface.

He sat on a bench overlooking the lake, slowly eating his lunch as if he didn't have a care in the world. Actually, he had a hundred things on his mind. His plans were getting closer to being a reality. Very, very shortly he would be rich. Rich beyond his wildest imagination, and he had discovered that he had a very large imagination.

A black kid sauntered up and sat down next to him. The kid wore a purple headband and no shirt.

Burke glanced over at Slats, leader of the gang he was using at the moment, then went back to eating his hot dog.

''Nice chain,'' he said, not even looking at the huge gold chain hanging around Slats's neck. The gold had to have cost the kid at least a thousand.

''Big,'' he added, still not looking at Slats. He took a large bite from his hot dog and continued to stare out over the lake as if he were alone.

''We're getting paid,'' Slats said. ''What's wrong with a little flossing, man?''

Burke snorted and wiped his mouth with a napkin

before turning to stare at the kid. "Floss too much, *man,* and the wrong people notice."

Slats squirmed under Burke's gaze, but said nothing.

"Maybe I better let somebody else ride in my little bankmobile. Maybe you'll end up like Cutter."

He didn't let his gaze drift from Slats' eyes. Finally the kid sighed, pulled the chain over his head, and then stuffed it in his pocket.

"Good," Burke said. "Hot dog?" He offered Slats the rest of his hot dog.

"Don't eat no pork shit," Slats said.

"This is turkey shit," Burke said.

Slats shrugged, took the hot dog and sniffed it. Then as Burke plucked a thick envelope from his jacket pocket, Slats took a bite.

Burke handed the envelope to Slats. "Singer will pick you and your men up. Stay precisely on schedule. And keep your group under control this time."

"How much we getting broke off?"

"More than you can imagine," Burke said. Then he glanced around to make sure no one was near. "Now, what's the buzz on this Steel guy?"

"Some crazy-ass fool running around in a tin suit," Slats said, taking another bite off the hot dog. "Sounds like a Tin Man on steroids."

Burke stared at Slats. "Never underestimate your enemy." Then he stood and turned to face Slats, giving the kid his meanest look. "Keep the gold out of sight. Eat the hot dog, don't be one."

Slats snorted as Burke turned and walked away. Then the kid finished the hot dog in one bite. Almost more than he could chew.

CHAPTER 31

UNCLE JOE EASED THE OLD JUNK VAN AROUND THE corner and stayed at the speed limit, letting the night and the life on the sidewalks pass them by like so many trees along a flowing river. Beside him on the passenger seat sat Lillie, her golden mane shining in the streetlights, her tongue slightly out of her mouth as she excitedly watched the passing sights. It was as if she were standing guard.

"Five nights," Sparks said over the intercom. Then she yawned and Uncle Joe smiled. He could see her back at the dome, her chair parked securely in front of her panel. "Five nights and still no sign of those weapons."

"Gettin' old, huh?" Steel said, leaning forward from the back of the van so he could look out between Uncle Joe and Lillie. He was in full armor, except for his helmet. And in the back of the van, facing the back doors, was his bike, tuned and ready to go.

"Well," Sparks said. "I like having the time to make improvements on my chair. That's been nice."

"Improvements?" Steel said, smiling at Uncle Joe, who only shook his head.

"Later," she said, again yawning. "What do you guys think about some wallpaper in here?"

Steel laughed. "Stay on point, Sparky. Something's gonna pop. And soon."

The armored Hummer rumbled around the corner of Hope Street and stopped, its lights off. The only light on the corner cast dark shadows over the Hummer, making it seem larger and even more dangerous than it already was.

The driver's door opened and Singer hopped out, dropping to the pavement without a sound. He wore a black jumpsuit, black shoes, and carried a black knapsack. At the moment he didn't have his mask on, but for this first stop he didn't need it.

He moved quickly to a manhole directly in front of the Hummer, bent down, and jacked it open. With a practiced move he dropped down inside, sliding the six feet down the metal ladder without touching a step as if he'd been working in manholes his entire life.

He quickly moved two steps to his right to a telephone junction box. He pulled a large explosive charge out of his knapsack and hung it on the box. With a quick check of the charge, he punched one button, then turned back to the ladder.

Back on the street he replaced the manhole cover, then without seeming to hurry, climbed back inside the Hummer and moved it forward so that one wheel rested squarely over the top of the manhole, holding the cover solidly in place.

Eight seconds later a large explosion rocked the street. Rockets of smoke fired out of the cracks around the manhole cover, and the Hummer rocked slightly.

But the manhole cover stayed in place.

Instantly the streetlights and all the building lights blinked and went out.

The neighborhood dropped into blackness.

Now only the faint light from other areas of the city lit the tops of the buildings. Almost no light reached the canyons of the streets.

Back in the dome Sparks finished a yawn just as her monitoring board lit up.

"What?" She jerked so hard she almost scooted herself out of her wheelchair. With a quick glance at her board she knew what had happened.

"Heads up," she said to Steel and Uncle Joe. "Something's cooking."

Her fingers flew over the computer keyboard, focusing in on the problem area.

"Give it to us," Steel said.

"The city's emergency services interlink shows a major telephone and power failure near Hope and Wilshire."

"We'll check it out," Steel said, his voice low and cold.

Sparks continued to type. "I'm zeroing in the LandSet. See if our eye in the sky spots anything."

She had managed to link into a private satellite in orbit over the Southern California area. In front of her a monitor showed an infrared satellite image of L.A. She punched it up closer so that it focused on the general area of the outage. It showed up as a dark area on the screen. Only the heat from vehicles moving marked the streets.

"This is big," she said. "Very big."

Steel and Uncle Joe didn't answer. But she knew they had heard her.

CHAPTER 32

TWO FLOORS UNDER THE FLASHY SHOWROOM OF Dantastic, Burke paced slowly back and forth on the tile floor in the high-tech room. At two monitors sat two ex-Navy Seals, Conrad and Stone. Both were computer experts, and experts at killing. Burke had hired them and two others. Granted, it was Daniels' money that paid them at the moment, but they reported only to him.

"Power's blown," Conrad said.

Burke stopped pacing and glanced over at Daniels with a smile.

"Time to make our major infomercial?" Daniels asked.

Burke only smiled, then turned to Conrad. "Do it."

In the junkyard dome, Sparks had every major band of police radio on, scanning constantly. The minute anyone knew what was happening, she would know. And if she could pinpoint anything on the satellite, she might even know sooner.

"Two Adam Seven," one police scanner squawked. "Possible 459 at Union Station. Respond—"

Suddenly the transmission was cut off.

"What?" Sparks said to herself, swinging her chair around to the scanners and making quick adjustments.

Only loud static greeted her efforts. Something was blocking all police bands.

She swung back to her main station. "Johnny? Do you read?"

Again nothing.

Someone was blocking *everything* in the area.

"Big," she said to herself. "Very big."

Her fingers flew over the keys of her computer. "Switching to FM," she said. "Shielded sideband. Do you read me now, Johnny?"

"I read you," Steel said, "five by five. What happened?"

"Jamming," Sparks said. "Big-time. Police frequencies are out, too. Something's going down."

"But where?" Steel asked.

"Good question," she said. "Very good question."

The Hummer rounded the darkened corner onto Hope and Sixth, moving down the middle of the street as if it didn't matter if another car were on the road or not. It was like a bully in a school yard. Nothing on the streets of this city could match this armored vehicle. And anything that dared go against it would quickly be destroyed.

Singer slowed the armored Hummer and stopped it facing a large, six-story-tall brick building. There were few windows, and the building itself gave the impression of being impenetrable.

Slats stared out from the passenger side. "We're home," he said, then quickly slid his mask into place.

Singer did the same, then clicked his mike. "Target in sight."

"Camera?" Conrad's voice came back to him.

Singer flipped a switch and with a hum the camera poked above the cab of the Hummer like a periscope from a submarine. On a small monitor built into the dashboard, Singer could see the camera pan first the street, then focus in on the front of the building.

"Proceed," Burke's voice said clearly over the radio.

"This is Papa Bear," Conrad said. "Go. Go."

Singer flipped a switch and the side port of the Hummer lowered and the sonic cannon came up and locked into position.

"Firing," he said, and punched another button.

With a loud boom, the cannon fired, rocking the Hummer slightly.

The battering ram of sound smashed into the brick and concrete wall of the huge building. The wall seemed to resist for only a fraction of a second, then it seemed to implode, crumbling in on itself.

A huge section of the wall from above smashed down, sending up a gigantic cloud of dust swirling into the blackness of the night.

The rumbling boom was heard by some within a mile of the explosion, but soon the sound was swallowed by the roar of the freeways and the low rumble of life.

And the cloud of dust was blown down the street by the gentle summer breeze.

Time in the geodesic dome seemed to move like a slow drip from a bathroom faucet. Nothing seemed to be happening, but Sparks knew that wasn't the case. It had been almost a minute since the power was knocked out. And even less since the jamming had started.

Something was going down.

She just had to find out what.

And where.

She worked frantically to find the emergency police band. They had more scouts out there. More eyes and ears. She needed to get back on line with them.

Suddenly on her satellite monitor a huge flash of heat source lit up the screen like someone flashing a light from inside the computer. A large explosion could be the only cause for that.

"Big disturbance at Sixth and Hope," she said, her voice breathless in her ears.

"Got it," Uncle Joe said. "On our way."

Her fingers brought up on the screen what was on that street corner.

"Oh, my God," she said, more to herself than Steel.

"Sparks?" Steel said. "What is it? What's there?"

Sparks shook her head. "Would you believe Los Angeles's biggest ATM?"

"The what?" Uncle Joe asked.

"The Federal Reserve Bank," Sparks said.

"Oh," was all Uncle Joe said in return.

Steel said nothing.

CHAPTER 33

MOLTEN DROPS OF STEEL DROPPED TO THE GROUND as the Hummer's laser bit into the metal of the bank vault. The brick and concrete wall that had covered the outside of the vault now lay in a pile on the sidewalk and the laser was having no problems at all cutting the steel.

From inside the building, two security guards appeared, guns drawn.

Balls of lightning streaked across the street and caught both guards squarely in the chests. Both exploded backward as if they were puppets attached to wires that had been suddenly yanked from above.

"I love this shit," Holdecker said, slapping the gun. Holdecker was Slats's second and the best shot of the group. He was the only one beside Slats with one of the special rifles.

"Be there," Slats said, his head going back and forth as he checked in both directions down the dark street.

The other five members of his gang also were at ready and were standing guard near the Hummer, regular pistols in their hands.

A huge chunk of steel suddenly broke loose and fell forward onto the pile of rubble on the sidewalk, sending up a second cloud of dust.

"Move your ass," Slats shouted to the others.

Holdecker and Slats both snapped on powerful Xenotech lights that cut through the dust, then led the others over the hot steel and into the vault.

The place was big, bigger than Slats had imagined. And it was filled with pallets stacked five high. All the pallets were full of bundles of newly printed hundred-dollar bills. Burke had told him there would be money in here, but not this much.

"Dammmmmnnnn!" Holdecker said, stopping and shining his light around the room. "There's a zillion dollars in here!"

"You know the drill," Slats said, indicating one of the pallets. He shouldered his rifle and snapped open his duffel bag. "Suck up all you can in ninety seconds."

"In position," Steel said as he stepped onto the darkened Hope Street. He moved forward, staying close to the side of a video arcade.

"Would you look at that," Sparks said in his ear.

He could see exactly what had caused her amazement. A large armored Hummer filled the middle of the street. The brick and concrete wall of the bank had been blown into rubble and the steel vault had been sliced open like it was nothing more than a thin slice of meat. There didn't seem to be anyone on the street.

"I'm going to get closer," Steel said.

"Six figures coming out of the vault," Sparks said after he'd only taken two steps.

"Got them," Steel said.

He pulled his hammer to his shoulder, flipped on the charge, and fired. He was still too far and the shot went slightly wide and into the bank wall beside the moving figures.

The impact of the fireball lit them up like a spotlight. They all wore black jumpsuits and black ski masks. All of them carried duffel bags, and two of them carried high-tech rifles.

"Ice his metal ass," Slats shouted.

He and Holdecker fired at the exact same moment, sending balls of lightning back at Steel.

One missed and smashed through the window of the video store behind him. The other caught him squarely in the chest.

He stood his ground against the impact as the ball of lightning bounced and smashed into a nearby pickup truck, catching it on fire.

"Too far away to use the magnet," Sparks said.

"The alloy in those guns is nonmagnetic," Steel said, moving forward.

"I knew that," Sparks said.

He lifted his hammer and fired again. This time he hit what he was aiming at, the huge bank sign over the sidewalk. With an explosion it snapped loose and dropped to the sidewalk, knocking down three of the six hooded figures.

Then he turned and fired at the Hummer's tires.

Direct hit, but no luck. The static bursts simply bounced off. One smashed into a parked car and caught it on fire.

"It's got armor like yours, Johnny," Sparks said, the worry clear in her voice.

"Let's try this," Steel said. He flipped the switch on his hammer fully back and fired again. Pellets smashed into the concrete around the gang members as they struggled to drag their friends toward the Hummer. Clouds of gas billowed up and around the gang, making them instantly cough.

"Tear gas, man!" Holdecker shouted.

"Jump the van," Slats shouted back. "Go!"

Steel ran out into the street as the six gang members moved in behind the Hummer and out of his line of fire.

"You're about to get the blue," Sparks said.

"I hear 'em," Steel said.

Slats shoved Holdecker into the Hummer and jumped in beside him, slamming the door behind them.

"Everyone accounted for *this* time?" Singer asked, glancing back at Slats.

"Counted," he said, then pointed down the street at the huge Steel man. "Who is that fool?"

Singer laughed. "A dead man," he said.

"Do him," Burke's voice said clearly over the communication line.

"Swing that sonic gun out," Singer said.

"Pleasure," Slats said, moving over and snapping the sonic gun out the side portal as the Hummer swung around.

"Fire," Singer said.

Slats yanked the gun down directly at the chest of the giant guy in tin and pulled the trigger.

The gun kicked slightly in his hand.

The huge tin man exploded up into the air like a feather blown off a table. He airmailed two cars and smashed back-first into a sidewalk news kiosk, shattering it as if a bomb had gone off inside the small structure. Magazines, books, newspapers, exploded out everywhere.

"He's on ice," Slats said, then slapped Holdecker's hand as nothing moved from the pile of wood and magazines.

CHAPTER 34

JACK SLID THE COP CAR SIDEWAYS ONTO HOPE Street just as the big guy dressed in steel from the other night was blown twenty feet through the air and into the newsstand.

"It's a damn war zone," rookie cop Peter said as he stared openmouthed at the remains of the front of the bank and the armored Hummer in the middle of the street.

"Take cover," Jack shouted. "That's the same machine that nailed those cop cars the other time."

He bailed out the driver's door and headed down the road behind a parked car.

Peter did the same on the other side just as a ball of lightning smashed into the squad car, filling it with flame and smashing out every window.

On the other side of the Hummer two more squad cars slid into roadblock formation. Peter could hear the approaching sound of a police chopper. They had whoever was breaking into the Federal Reserve surrounded. Now all they had to do was hold them.

A bright light flashed from the sky as the chopper cleared the top of the building and sent its searchlight right onto the Hummer. Suddenly a ball of lightning shot up and hit the chopper, faster than Peter could follow.

The chopper valiantly tried to get away, but almost instantly the insides of the chopper were filled with flames.

What followed was like a nightmare that Peter had hoped he'd never see. But now it was coming true.

There were two quick explosions inside the chopper, then, as if in slow motion, it nosed in toward the street, heading directly for where Jack crouched behind the car.

"Jack!" Peter shouted into the roar of explosions and helicopter motor, but the sound was swallowed almost as it left his mouth.

Jack crouched behind a parked car, ready to fire at anything that looked like it was part of the robbery crew. In all his years he'd seen a lot of strange stuff, but this Hummer robbery crew was the strangest.

And the most deadly.

Suddenly the world around him went crazy.

Their patrol car took a direct hit, flipped over, and exploded. Then a fireball shot up at the police chopper overhead, catching it squarely.

The chopper tried to pull away, then the insides burst into flames and the bird nosed down.

Right at him.

And there wasn't a damn thing he could do about it. The thought that he was going to die crossed his mind.

Suddenly it felt as if a train had rammed him, picking him up and tossing him down the sidewalk like a rag doll.

Instinctively he tucked and rolled, banging his shoulder hard, but somehow protecting his head. He rolled to a stop and suddenly there was this huge weight on top of him. Then the world around him exploded in flames, and the sidewalk shook like a seven-point earthquake.

Then, almost as quickly as it happened, it was over.

The weight on top of him lifted, and he sat up.

A moment before he had been buried within the burning remains of the police chopper and half a dozen parked cars.

The man in the steel suit slowly pushed himself to his feet, then looked into Jack's eyes, offering him a hand up.

Jack could tell he was hurting. And his chin under the mask was bleeding. But the dark eyes were what caught Jack's attention. They were the eyes of a man who had saved his life. And he'd never forget them. He took the strong grasp of the man's hand and let him pull him to his feet.

The man in the steel suit nodded to Jack, then turned and ran around the corner.

A moment later Peter was over to him, the kid's worried face staring at him. "Jack? Jack? You all right?"

"I think so," he said.

Down the street the Hummer turned and, with a blast from the weapon on its roof, smashed through the two cop cars and disappeared around the corner.

Hope Street glowed orange from the burning fires, a war zone in the middle of the city.

"You all right, big fellow?" Sparks asked as Steel headed for his motorcycle.

"I'll live," he said. But in reality he was hurting. And hurting bad. The sonic blast had bruised or maybe broken some ribs. And the dive to save the cop had cost him dearly in pain. He was going to be lucky to not have punctured a lung, from the way the burning in his chest felt.

With a quick twist he was aboard the motorcycle and heading away.

"Blue bubble on your tail," Sparks said. "Turn right on Flower Street and gun it."

He swung the bike around onto Flower. Behind him the squad car followed, fishtailing for a moment, then coming on strong.

Steel flipped a small switch on his handlebar and a broad spray of very sharp, very long tacks sprayed out behind him. Tacks designed to stand on end when dropped.

The squad car didn't even see them. A moment later all four tires blew, almost instantly. The car slid sideways, spun once, and came to a stop.

"Beside you," Sparks said.

A motorcycle cop came in hard from a side street and swung in behind Steel.

A block later Sparks said, "He's closing on you."

Steel yanked his hammer out of its back sling, flipped it sideways and set it for laser. Ahead was a street cleaner, its fine spray of water covering the road ahead of its swirling brushes.

Steel timed the shot exactly right, slicing a long laser cut down the side of the water tank.

The tank was gutted like a dead fish, and water sprayed out in a huge wave.

The motorcycle cop couldn't have avoided it if he'd tried.

The torrent of water caught him in a direct broadside, knocking him sideways and up onto a lawn. His bike jammed against a low brick wall and stopped instantly. The cop went over the handlebars, landing headfirst in a huge shrub that decorated the front of an office building.

"You're clear," Sparks said. "Just hang in there a little longer."

"You steer," Steel said.

"Go left onto Garland," Sparks said after a moment. "You'll see the rabbit hole. You should make it before your new company catches you."

Steel almost laid the bike over on its side as he turned the corner onto Garland. Just as Sparks said, there ahead of him was Uncle Joe's junk van, its back end open, its tailgate a fraction of an inch above the ground.

Almost standing on the brakes, he steered the bike up inside, stopping just before smashing into the cab wall of the van.

Behind him the door slammed shut.

A moment later a cop car, lights flashing, sirens blaring, streaked past the old junk van, paying it no attention at all.

John Henry somehow managed to climb off the motorcycle, but he wasn't sure how he did it.

CHAPTER 35

IN THE SECRET HIGH-TECH LAB TWO STORIES BELOW the Dantastic lobby, Burke paced behind Conrad, whose fingers punched keys like he was trying for the world record in typing.

Finally Conrad paused, then shook his head.

"He stopped transmitting before I could triangulate," Conrad said without turning around to look at Burke. "But I got some parameters."

"Good," Burke said. "Find his home base."

Burke moved over behind the other man at the console. "Stone, you got the tapes?"

Stone turned and with a smile held up five videocassettes. "Copied, rewound, and ready to play."

Burke nodded. "Get them to the television stations as quickly as possible. And make sure they can't be traced."

Without another word Stone got to his feet and headed for the elevator.

Burke dropped down into a chair.

The bait was out.

Now all he had to do was wait for the fish to bite.

*   *   *

In a cinder-block building tucked behind a Chevron garage in southern Georgia, a television ran the attack on the Federal Reserve, weapons fire, helicopter crash, and all.

Six men dressed in Army fatigues, heads shaved close, watched. Behind them a large Nazi flag hung from the wall above thirty rifles and AK-47s.

After the announcer came back on, one man named Brian turned to a younger skinhead. "I want some of them weapons."

The younger man shrugged. "How?"

The older skinhead stepped toward the younger, his face a mask of anger. "I don't care how. Just get 'em."

The morning was breaking clear in western Africa as CNN broadcast the news of the attack on the Federal Reserve.

Two French mercenaries sat, legs up, watching. One was cleaning his AK-47. The other sipped on a mug of soup.

After the newscast finished, the mercenary with the mug turned to the other. "Find out who makes those new toys."

The other only nodded and kept cleaning his gun.

Colombian drug lord Territin snapped open his cell phone. Spread out in front of him was a lavish dinner, prepared by his chef. The calm Caribbean waters of the bay gently rocked his yacht, but at the moment he was paying no attention to either his dinner or the beautiful evening.

"Did you see the newscast from Los Angeles?" he asked.

He nodded to the response on the other end of the

phone call, then said, "Find out how we get them. Use the Internet, stupid. Pronto."

He snapped the phone closed and then went back to eating, shaking his head at the stupidity of his underlings.

CHAPTER 36

INSIDE THE GEODESIC DOME IN THE JUNKYARD, Sparks and Uncle Joe helped John Henry take off his armor. Underneath he was bloody in a dozen places, and ugly bruises were forming in a dozen more. Almost every time he moved, John Henry winced.

"Oh, my god," Sparks said, taking one piece of armor and tossing it aside. "You may be steel on the outside, but you're still flesh and blood underneath."

Uncle Joe helped John Henry off with his chest plate. "Too much blood, looks like."

"I'm okay," John Henry said, wincing as Uncle Joe unhooked another part of the armor. "It's just a few scratches."

"Oh, cut the macho bullshit," Sparks said, glaring at him. "I'd be surprised if you don't have at least two broken ribs."

John Henry took a deep and obviously painful breath. "You may be right, Sparks." Then he shook his head, as he stared at drops of his own blood on the concrete floor. "I don't know if I can do this."

Uncle Joe snorted. "It's hard going," he said, not looking at John Henry, but instead concentrating on one chunk of armor. "No question. Just like ol' John Henry went through."

Sparks glared at Uncle Joe. "Yeah," she said, her voice low and cold. "And we all know what happened to him."

Uncle Joe didn't seem to notice her angry tone. He just nodded and kept working to remove the armor. "Yeah, he died pounding steel. But he beat that ol' steam drill."

"But he died doing it," Sparks said, not even trying to hide the anger in her voice.

Uncle Joe laughed. "Can't argue with you there," he said. " 'Course he didn't have *you* to help him."

Sparks blinked at him, then shook her head in disgust. "That's got nothing to—"

John Henry held up his hand for them to stop. "Can I get some water?"

Uncle Joe patted John Henry carefully on the shoulder between bruises, then stood and headed for the sink.

Sparks wheeled around so that she could reach more of John Henry's wounds with a soft antiseptic pad. "We're going to have to wrap those ribs."

He nodded. "I'll get them checked in a few days. Got too much work to do first."

She snorted. "You're as crazy as that old man."

Behind her the police scanner lit up again, this time with a description of Steel.

"They got a warrant out for me?" John Henry asked, his attitude getting quickly more depressed.

"For the man in steel," she corrected him. "Some of the cops think you're part of that gang, most likely since you had the same weapons."

"Wonderful," he said softly.

"There's more," she said. "Somehow most of the television stations got videotapes of the robbery. CNN is running the tapes every half hour."

Uncle Joe handed John Henry a huge paper cup full of water, and he downed half of it in two large gulps. Then he paused and looked at Sparks.

"I have a feelin' Burke is down with this somehow."

Sparks nodded. "It would be logical," she said.

He took another drink of water, then said, "I've gotta find those weapons."

He crumpled the cup and lobbed it at the trash can across the dome. Of course, he missed.

"Excuse me," Sparks said, moving her chair up directly in front of him. "What you've got to do is get some sleep. Give those ribs a little time to set."

John Henry nodded to her and pulled on a sweat jacket and pants. Uncle Joe helped him slip on and tie his tennis shoes. Then John Henry slowly turned and headed for the door.

At the entrance he turned and pointed his finger at Sparks.

She pointed back and he smiled, then left.

"You're really leaning on him," Sparks said as she turned back to Uncle Joe.

"At the mill," he said, bending down and picking up pieces of Steel's suit, "I noticed how iron that went through the hottest fire made the best-quality steel at the other end."

"*If* it comes out the other end," Sparks said, glaring at the old man. "Why are you pressing him so hard?"

" 'Cause I love him," Uncle Joe said without looking at her. "And what he's trying to do. He's a lot of man, but nothing's bigger than his heart."

He moved over to drop the armor into a cleaning vat,

then said, "Same reason I love you, Sparky."

She looked up, surprised, right into Uncle Joe's deep brown eyes. And at that moment she understood, maybe for the first time, what John Henry Irons was all about.

CHAPTER 37

CONRAD STOOD UP FROM HIS CHAIR AND MOVED over to where Burke sat at a television screen watching the news. So far CNN had run the story of the robbery twelve times, each time showing the world his new weapons. And each time those weapons got airtime he knew he'd hooked another possible customer somewhere in the world.

"Sir," Conrad said, handing Burke a slip of paper with an address written on it.

Burke stared at it for a moment, then smiled up at the stern face of Conrad. "Well done."

Burke rubbed the scar on the side of his face, then slid forward, picked up a phone, and punched in a number off a pad beside the phone. He'd been ready to make this call all day long.

A moment later the phone on the other end was picked up.

"Good evening, Sergeant," Burke said to the officer who answered. "Would you like to know where to find the fancy weapon that brought down your helicopter?"

A moment later Burke had read the address to the sergeant and hung up.

Then kicking his feet up on the foot rest, he returned to watching the news and his free worldwide advertising campaign.

As on most nights, Grandma Odessa's kitchen was warm and smelled wonderful. It was as if the smell of baked bread and roasting turkey had permanently soaked into everything in the room.

Tonight the smell of cheese added to the other thick aromas, making John Henry realize how hungry he was.

And how tired.

Grandma Odessa stood at the counter, hunched over a notebook, writing with a pencil. When he entered she glanced up and whispered, "Evening."

"Soufflé?" John Henry whispered back while moving over and kissing her lightly on her forehead.

Grandma Odessa nodded, then whispered, "Gonna get it right if it kills me." She looked up from her notebook and at his face. "What happened to your chin?"

"Oh," John Henry said, his hand coming up to the sore spot on his chin. "I bumped into something."

"Did ya?" Grandma Odessa whispered, looking up into his eyes. Then she looked back down at her notebook, seeming to focus on it. But then, before John Henry could move on, she asked, "See any of that big robbery stuff on the TV?"

"On TV?" John Henry asked, making sure to keep his voice low. "No, ma'am. Haven't been near a TV tonight."

Grandma Odessa nodded, then without looking up she said, "Times is hard on the streets. Everybody feels like this big black cloud's hanging over 'em. Know what I mean?"

She looked up into his eyes.

"I do," he whispered.

"Only hope seems to be that Steel boy. He's sure a big drink o' water. Big. Tall. Like you."

"Is he?" John Henry said, turning to look for something to eat in the refrigerator. After a moment he closed the door with nothing in his hands. He was just too tired to even find himself something to eat.

"Well. Think I'm gonna get me some sleep."

Grandma Odessa stared at John Henry, then stepped up to him. "What's that in your ear, son?"

"In my. . .?" John Henry whispered, his hand going to his ear and finding the tiny hearing aid. "Oh, forgot about it."

He moved his hand away, leaving the ear receiver in just in case Sparks had to get hold of him. "It's a little hearing aid thing that I'm trying out."

"You never had no hearing problems," Grandma Odessa whispered, staring at him.

"Huh?" he said.

"I said you never had no—"

John Henry smiled at her as she caught his joke.

She poked him on the arm, hitting one of his sore spots.

"Now don't you play with me, boy."

She paused, glanced at her notebook, then looked straight into John Henry's eyes. "I want to know the truth. Are you—"

Suddenly the back door smashed inward, banging against the wall.

At that same moment a man dressed all in black crashed through the kitchen window, rolling once across the kitchen floor. The man wore a black-visored helmet and carried a rifle in his hands.

Grandma Odessa reacted instantly, as if she'd been fighting off intruders her entire life.

She grabbed the rolling pin off the counter and backhanded the man in black as he came up.

The thunk echoed in the kitchen as the rolling pin connected with his face plate and sent him over backward. He smashed into the stove, knocking the door open.

Inside the soufflé dropped into a flat mass of brown.

John Henry grabbed the first man in black through the kitchen door and whipped him around and into the wall. Another entered from the front room while a second came in the back door.

"Police!" one shouted. "Freeze!"

John Henry stood ready to fight, but suddenly the L.A. Police Swat team logo was very clear on their black uniforms.

He froze, slowly raising his hands.

Grandma Odessa glanced at him, then did the same.

"On the ground," one of the cops said to John Henry, indicating the floor with the barrel of his rifle. "Now!"

Martin was suddenly shoved into the room by another man in black.

"Grandma?" Martin said, his eyes wide with fear. "What's happenin'?"

"Do it!" the one facing John Henry said, again pointing to the ground.

"I'm down. I'm down," John Henry said, holding his hands over his head while kneeling. "Be cool."

Another cop moved into the kitchen. He waved a paper in front of Grandma Odessa. "This is a search warrant."

The new arrival turned to two of the men and nodded. They disappeared back into the house.

John Henry could feel his wrists yanked behind his

back and he groaned at the pain in his arms and ribs. "Take it easy, would you?"

"John Henry Irons," the man kneeling beside him said. "You're under arrest for suspicion of armed robbery, assault, and possession of illegal weapons."

"Johnny?" Grandma Odessa said, her voice firm, yet clearly full of worry. "What are they talking about?"

A black-uniformed cop came back into the kitchen holding one of the heat-pulse rifles. John Henry couldn't believe what he was seeing. How did that get in the house? Someone must have planted it.

He turned his head and glanced at Martin. From the stare on Martin's face, the kid had never seen the weapon before, either.

"Sir," the cop with the gun said, holding it for the cop in charge to see. "It was in the basement."

The man nodded. "He definitely fits the description."

"Description for what?" Grandma Odessa demanded, stepping up and looking the cop square in the eye.

"To be that dude they're callin' Steel, ma'am."

Grandma Odessa glanced at Martin, then stepped back as John Henry was read his rights and hauled out the back door.

CHAPTER 38

THE POLICE STATION SMELLED OF SWEAT AND PISS. And by nine in the morning, the entire station was already ten degrees too hot for any sort of human comfort. A rumbling air-conditioning system tried to fight back the heat of the day outside, but without luck. There were just too many open doors and people.

By midnight the night before, John Henry had been booked and fingerprinted, then questioned for half an hour before being shoved into a cell. There, on a bench far too short for him to lie down on, he'd managed to sleep off and on. At seven in the morning a cop carrying a breakfast of toast, runny eggs, and orange juice had woke him up.

The food had actually tasted good and helped him feel a little better. And his ribs were feeling better, too. Maybe they weren't broken after all, but only cracked. A few more days and he might actually be able to move without flinching in pain.

Two hours after breakfast he was escorted out of his cell and into a lineup, facing a black window that was obviously a two-way mirror. This room was flooded with light and smelled like someone had thrown up the night before. In the huge window/mirror he could see his reflection. He looked rumpled and tired. Just like he felt.

Imagine that.

On either side of him were five other tall black men, all looking either annoyed or bored as they faced the black window and whoever was on the other side.

In his ear Sparks said, "Tell me when you're back in your cell and can talk," she said. "I got some news."

He didn't dare answer her. Instead he just stood looking as bored as he could, staring at himself in the mirror.

Inside the darkened viewing area on the other side of the mirror, a police detective stood next to the young couple that had been mugged six nights before. Dorie Kearny and Jon Merchant. Dorie had her hair pulled back and tied, and both looked like they had dressed quickly.

And both looked very annoyed about being in the hot, smelly room.

The detective, a man named Alaska, leaned into a mike. "Number one, step forward."

The man on the couple's far left stepped forward. He didn't look happy.

The young couple looked at him, then Jon shook his head no. "Not tall enough."

"Step back, number one," Detective Alaska said. "Number two, front and center."

Number two stepped forward, laughing to himself. "You got it, man," he said. "I always wanted to be in *Chorus Line*."

"Put a lid on it, number two," Detective Alaska said.

Dorie turned to Alaska. "You know, Detective, he was very kind to us. I'd hate to—"

The detective shook his head and sighed. "I know, ma'am. But serious crimes have been committed."

Jon glanced at the men in the lineup, then turned to Detective Alaska. "Two's not big enough." Then he took a deep breath. "Officer, the man who helped us was on the right side of the law." He glanced at his companion, then went on. "And he's not up there."

"Are you sure?" Alaska asked, staring first at Jon and then Dorie, his annoyance not far below the surface.

Both of them nodded yes.

"All right," he said, moving over and opening the door to the small room. "Thanks for coming."

They moved out and both almost ran for the front door as Detective Alaska stood shaking his head.

Then he turned and yelled down the crowded hall. "Jack? C'mere."

The senior cop who had been driving the patrol car the night before stepped around the corner and up to the detective.

"You saw him real good," Alaska said.

"I did," Jack said. "Real good."

"Then get in there and find him," Alaska said, indicating the door to the lineup room.

Jack opened it and walked in front of the six tall men. He went clear to the far right with number six and stared him in the eye.

"Not him," Jack said, shaking his head.

He moved to stand in front of number five.

"Nope," he said after a moment.

Then he stopped in front of number four.

The guy had a cut on his chin and Jack knew instantly he was the one who had saved his life the night before. And the one who had tried to stop the bank robbers.

He kept his face calm, as if he'd just gotten a good

hand of cards, then shook his head. "Not this one, either."

The man had saved his life. This was the least he could do for the guy.

Ten minutes later John Henry was back in his cell.

For some reason the cop he'd saved had refused to identify him in the lineup. Someday, a long time from now, if he got the chance, he'd thank the guy.

The guard who had escorted him turned and moved away from the cell.

"Okay," John Henry said softly, yet loud enough for Sparks to hear through the small microphone in the tiny earpiece. "I'm back in my cell."

"Why won't they let you come home?" Sparks asked, her voice sounding worried.

"They're holding me for questioning," he said. "NSA's flying Colonel David in."

"Maybe he'll be able to help," Sparks said.

John Henry shook his head and looked around to make sure no one was close enough to hear him talking. "Don't count on it. Did you do the checks I suggested?"

"Yeah," Sparks said. "The TV stations said the tapes of the robbery were sent anonymously. Big-time infomercial: high-tech weapons, not available in any store. And if you act now—"

"How does the buyer make contact?" John Henry asked, breaking into her monologue.

She laughed. "In this day and age, only one way. The Internet."

"I thought so," he said. "Did you find it?"

Again she laughed. "Remember who you're talking to here. Of course I did. But the bad news is that the big auction is going down in eleven hours."

"They give a location?"

"Nothing closer than Southern California," she said. "The exact location will come at the last minute."

"Hold on," he said. He stood and moved over to the door. The guard was down the hall a ways.

"Hey, guard," he shouted.

"What?" the guy said, moving down the hallway toward John Henry.

"Could you get that detective for me?"

The guard laughed. "He'll be in to see you when he's ready, not the other way around."

Still laughing, the guard turned and headed back to his chair at the end of the hall.

"Sparky, I need to get out of here."

"Granted," she said. "We need help from higher up. And that may take a while."

"We don't have a while," John Henry said.

"Working on it," Sparks said. "Just sit tight."

John Henry laughed and glanced around at the ten-by-ten cell. "Sit tight, she says. As if I can go someplace."

CHAPTER 39

THE OUTER OFFICE OF DISTRICT ATTORNEY MITCHELL Litt occupied a large corner on the top floor of the five-story Simpson Building. Large plants filled the corners, and dark leather couches were centered under large oil paintings on two walls.

A huge oak desk filled the wall across from the glass doors into the hall. A secretary in her thirties sat behind the desk, working intently at a computer screen. Her long brown hair was pulled back and up and her polished fingernails clicked on the keys of the computer like a light rain on a tin roof.

Uncle Joe, carrying a package and an electronic signature board, entered the room as if he'd done so a hundred times. He knew the best way to get anything was to act as if what he was after was normal.

He was dressed in a brown delivery-man suit and carried an official brown envelope addressed to the district attorney. He looked the delivery man part and if he acted the part, he would never be questioned.

"Package for Mitchell Litt," he said, glancing at his board as if to check the name.

"I'll sign for it," the woman behind the desk said, reaching out with one hand without taking her eyes from the screen.

"Can't on this one," he said, again studying his board as if that told him the reason why not. He looked up into her somewhat annoyed gaze and shrugged. "That's what it says here," he said, indicating his board. "Sorry."

She frowned, punched a key on her computer, then clicked the intercom. "Sir, a package for you to sign for."

"Right out," the voice said.

A moment later the door behind the secretary's desk opened, and the small frame of Mitchell Litt appeared. Uncle Joe had seen him a number of times in news reports, but never in person. He was much shorter than he looked on TV.

"Sorry to bother you, sir," Uncle Joe said. "Just need a quick signature right here." He pointed to a spot on the electronic pad.

The district attorney didn't even question, just signed and handed the board back to Uncle Joe.

Uncle Joe glanced at the signature, then smiled and handed the package to the district attorney.

"Have a good day," Uncle Joe said, then turned and headed for the door. He managed to contain his laugh until he got in the elevator. The district attorney would open the package to discover he might be a winner of Publisher's Clearinghouse. Of course, he wouldn't win, especially since Sparks had made up the form.

Outside the building, standing in the shade of a sidewalk tree, Uncle Joe hooked up the electronic board to a cell phone. Then punched two buttons. "You gettin' his signature?" he asked, wiping the sweat from his forehead.

Sparks's voice came back strong in his ear. "That's a big ten-four. Comin' in clear."

"Great," Uncle Joe said. "Now I can get out of this monkey suit and get me something to drink."

"Go for it," Sparks said. "Step two under way."

Back in the front office of District Attorney Mitchell Litt, the phone rang and the secretary picked it up, still not taking her eyes from the computer screen. Then suddenly she stopped. "Please hold," she said, then punched the intercom. "Sir, the mayor's office is on line one."

"Thank you," Mitchell Litt said, then picked up the phone and identified himself.

Sparks double-checked to make sure Litt's voice was being recorded, then said, "Hello, sir. I'm Connie Lavine with the mayor."

"Yes, Connie," he said as if he'd known her for some time, even though no Connie Lavine worked for the mayor.

Sparks managed to not laugh. "I know this is short notice," she said, "but the mayor wanted to know if you were free this afternoon?"

"Well," Litt said, "it *is* pretty short notice, but I certainly could try to move things around. I could be free by one o'clock."

"Great," Sparks said. "Don't do anything yet. I'll call back in a few minutes to confirm."

"Fine," he said.

Sparks hung up, laughing. "This is way too much fun," she said to herself. "Way too much. Now for step three."

It took her less than ten minutes to set up the voice translation program using the district attorney's voice.

Then she called the jail where they were holding John Henry.

"You're holding a prisoner there," she said, the computer translating her voice into district attorney Litt's. "His name is John Henry Irons. It *is* pretty short notice, but I want him free by one o'clock."

"Of course, sir," the guard on the other end of the phone line said. "But I'll need—"

"Written authorization," Sparks said in the DA's voice. "Of course. It's coming over your fax now with my signature on it."

Then she hung up, chuckling to herself. "Way too much fun."

CHAPTER 40

AT TEN MINUTES AFTER TWO IN THE AFTERNOON, John Henry climbed into the back of Uncle Joe's junk van around the corner from the jail. With a quick move, Uncle Joe took the van out into traffic and five minutes later they had determined to both their satisfactions that they weren't being followed.

Four hours later John Henry was in armor, and they were back on the street, ready to go.

"Sparks," John Henry said, from the back of the van. "We're cruisin' Alameda, passing—"

"Union Station," Sparks said. "I gotcha."

"Good," John Henry said. "Have you connected with the colonel?"

"Anonymously," she said, "through a satellite link so they couldn't trace it here."

"Did he believe you?" John Henry asked.

Sparks laughed. "Of course. He's in town and they're holding at the police heli-pad until you're sure it's really going down and I can give them a hard target."

John Henry nodded, then leaned forward to watch out

the front window. As he did so the pain in his side made him gasp.

"Those ribs still bothering you?" Sparks said. "My monitors show your respiration's still funky."

"Naaaw," he said.

"Naaaw," she repeated back, making her voice sound deep and very close to John Henry's. "We can handle it. We're men."

She dropped the imitating tone. "Johnny, I'm worried about you. Going into this with less than—"

She suddenly stopped.

"Sparky?" John Henry said.

"Hang on a second," she said. "I got something."

John Henry made himself take a slow, shallow breath and let it out.

"Off Eagle Rock Boulevard," she said. "North of the river. Just after sundown."

"What's there?" John Henry asked as Uncle Joe switched lanes quickly and made a sharp left turn.

"I'm scopin' the image from LandSat. Looks like some kind of old factory."

With another sharp corner Uncle Joe turned the old van up onto the freeway.

"Okay, Sparky," John Henry said, glancing over Uncle Joe's shoulder. "We're—"

"Northbound on the Hollywood to Pasadena," she said. "I'm calling the cavalry."

There was a click in John Henry's ear and she was gone. He felt very alone without her talking in his head.

Five minutes later she still hadn't come back and John Henry knew something was wrong. Very wrong. But there was nothing he could do now. They had to get to that warehouse.

Otherwise there was no telling how many thousands would die if those guns got into the wrong hands.

*   *   *

The sunset over the city on this hot summer evening had been beautiful. The sky had filled with orange and reds, lighting up the smog and high clouds with bright colors that seemed to glow with life of their own. John Henry just hoped he would be around tomorrow to see what that one looked like.

The old abandoned mill was tucked in an area between a steel storage yard and the Los Angeles River. They made a quick drive-by, then Uncle Joe got the van inside the steel yard and hidden.

Steel had moved into a better position, closer to the mill, and then they waited for the sun to go down.

Now Steel stood in thick cover watching the mill through a night scope, sending the images back to Uncle Joe in the truck.

A Navy Seal-type guard patrolled the yard with two Dobermans. Five black limos were parked near the main entrance of the old mill.

"Those limos seem a tad out of place," Uncle Joe said in Steel's ear.

"You got that right," Steel whispered back. He took as deep a breath as his sore ribs would allow, then let it out slowly to calm his nerves.

"Okay," he said to Uncle Joe, "it's about time. If you can't raise Sparky in the next two minutes, get to the colonel through the satellite link."

"Gotcha," Uncle Joe said. "Be careful. You ain't Superman. And you ain't gettin' paid."

Without another word Steel moved off toward the old mill, moving from one covered area to another. At the edge of the mill complex he stopped.

The Seal with the two Dobermans was patrolling near the limos, heading Steel's way slowly.

Steel unstrapped his hammer and quickly adjusted the

sonic switch. With a quick press of a switch it emitted
a very high-pitched squeal. Quickly Steel adjusted it
even higher until suddenly the Dobermans started whin-
ing, pawing at their ears.

"Sorry, guys," Steel whispered.

"What's the matter with you?" the guard said as the
dogs suddenly yanked him off in the opposite direction
from Steel, pulling him out of sight around the building.

Keeping the hammer in his hand, he quickly climbed
over the fence, dashed across the small open area and
up an old flight of stairs.

There, working his way along the walkway in the
dark, he found a mezzanine window.

Inside was a huge room, with a high roof and concrete
floor. Large wooden support pillars stood like trees
spaced evenly around the huge room.

Through the dirt of the window John Henry could see
ten men, obviously the ones who had come in the limos.
A very short man and three other guards all faced Burke,
and they were all carrying sonic weapons.

"Thought so," Steel said. He knew that Burke had to
be behind all this. But having it confirmed didn't make
him feel any better. Not in the slightest.

He flipped a small switch on the hammer and the head
fanned out into a small dish antenna. He aimed it
through the window and instantly the voice of Burke
came clearly to his ears. Burke's words would also be
transmitted back to the van and recorded.

"With the help of Mr. Daniels here," Burke said, indicating the short man in the expensive suit, "I've already made quite a few of these dandy little toys." He
indicated the sonic rifles in the hands of the guards.

There was a murmuring in the group watching, but
Steel couldn't pick up anything anyone said.

"You've all seen these weapons at work on TV,"

Burke went on. "Tonight I'm going to present a little firsthand demo."

Suddenly a voice behind Steel said, "Excuse me."

Steel whipped around, pulling up the hammer to fire as he moved.

But he was too late.

The guard fired the sonic rifle at point-blank range.

The impact felt to Steel like he'd walked squarely into a wall. And the pain from his ribs shocked him in its intensity.

The force of the blast knocked Steel backward and through the window.

He tried to break his fall by grabbing at anything he could see. But nothing stopped him completely as he crashed through the old window and then the wood of the mezzanine floor.

He dropped for what seemed like forever. Finally the hard concrete floor of the mill knocked the wind out of him and sent waves of pain through his chest.

"So welcome Mr. Warm and Fuzzy himself," Burke said to his suddenly very upset audience of weapons buyers, pointing at Steel. Then he turned to Steel. "Took you long enough."

Steel had somehow managed to hold on to his hammer. He rolled over as quickly as his ribs allowed and brought the hammer up, pointing it directly at Burke.

Burke only smiled, the ugly scar moving on his face like a red worm crawling over his cheek and into his eye.

"Uh-uh-uhhh," he said, waving his finger back and forth at Steel like a teacher scolding a misbehaving child. "You *might* want to think about that."

He turned and pointed toward a door on the other side of the open mill area. There a very angry Sparks sat in her wheelchair, glaring at Burke. Two guards had weapons pointed directly at her head.

"Sparks?" he said.

"Now ain't that touching," Burke said.

Steel sighed, looked at Burke, then dropped his hammer with a loud thud. Across the room Sparks got even angrier, but said nothing.

Burke shook his head as he walked over beside Steel and picked up the hammer. "See," he said, facing Steel. "That's the difference between us: I'd kiss her sorry ass good-bye and worry about myself."

Burke turned. "Singer, watch our guest."

A thick, overmuscled man stepped forward and pointed a sonic cannon directly at Steel.

"Okay, gentlemen," Burke said, stepping back to face his buyers. "Here's the deal: I can supply you with weapons like these on a sort of permanent lease."

One of the buyers with a shaved head stepped forward. "Lease? What the hell you talkin'?"

Another more classy-looking man nodded. "I only buy, mate. Flat-out."

"And you're welcome to do that," Burke said. "But unfortunately these weapons are highly sophisticated electronic devices that require specialized maintenance and *recharging*." He smiled at his audience. "Only I will be able to do that for you."

"Only we," the short man named Daniels said, stepping up beside Burke. "Only *we* can do that for you."

Burke nodded, then pulled a smaller version of the sonic rifle from his side and turned to face Daniels.

"No," he said. "I think I said it the correct way."

The burst of ball lightning cut into the short man's chest and he screamed, then tumbled over backward.

Burke stuck the weapon back in his holster as he

walked over and looked down at the clearly dead Daniels.

"First time his suit has ever been wrinkled," Burke said. "Too bad, too.

"Now," he said, turning back to his clearly troubled audience, "shall we get back to it?"

CHAPTER 41

"OH, MAN," UNCLE JOE SAID. "WE'RE IN SOME DEEP shit."

He'd just heard Steel say Sparks's name aloud, which meant she was in there with them, captured. And even if he could get through to Colonel David immediately, it would take the colonel at least five minutes to get to the mill.

"Deep shit," he said again.

He grabbed the microphone, but before he could even start to hook into the satellite to call the colonel, the back door of the van was yanked open.

He turned, reaching for his pistol, but was blinded by a bright light squarely in the face. The only thing he could see through the light was the barrel of a very nasty-looking rifle.

"Come on out of the truck, old man," a voice said. "And just leave the gun right where it is."

Slowly Uncle Joe crawled out.

His captor was one of Burke's professional guards. The guy carried one of the fancy weapons John Henry

and Sparks had talked about. A weapon he definitely
didn't want to get shot with.

The guy moved between him and the truck and indicated with the rifle that Uncle Joe should move toward
the mill.

Like a flash of gold, Lillie jumped from the truck,
hitting the guy squarely in the back with both her front
paws. She growled furiously, her weight and the surprise
of her attack driving the guard to the ground.

Uncle Joe took two quick steps and kicked the guy
once, solidly in the groin, following through the kick
like he'd seen punters do it on television in football
games. The guard doubled over and his face turned
bright red. Uncle Joe yanked the gun from the guy's
hands. As the guy tried to stand Uncle Joe clubbed him
with the butt of the rifle against the side of the head.

The guard went down like a sack of concrete.

And stayed there.

"That's gotta hurt," Uncle Joe muttered.

He took a quick look around, then moved over and
rubbed Lillie's ears as he tried to catch his breath.

"I owe you a steak, Lil," he said.

She wagged her tail.

"Okay," he said. "Now can you help me tie this guy
up and drag him over behind that pile of rebar?"

Again Lillie only wagged her tail.

"Didn't think so," he said.

Steel had watched, amazed and shocked, as Burke shot
down his own partner. Obviously Burke had completely
lost all sense of reality. And there didn't seem to be an
ounce of good left in the guy, if there ever had been.

Across the room Steel caught Sparks' attention. With
a quick hand motion he told her to be ready. He didn't

know if she could help, but she could dive out of that chair and take cover if shooting started.

She nodded back just once.

"All right, gentlemen," Burke said, facing his weapons buyers. "Who's going to sign up first?"

"It's blackmail," one of the buyers said, stepping forward slightly.

"No," Burke said, shaking his head. "It's just damn good business."

"So how much?" the buyer asked.

Burke snorted. "Millions, of course. But hey, I'm sure you can all afford it."

The buyer frowned. "You don't need our money," he said. "With these weapons you can steal all you want."

"True," Burke said, stepping toward the buyer, who didn't flinch. "But this really isn't about money, now is it?"

The guy stared Burke squarely in the eye. "You'll be the illegal arms supplier to the world. Now I see your game. You want the power."

Burke laughed. "Now there's an idea." He turned away, moving back to a position near his guards.

Burke lit up a cigar, taking his time, playing out the moment. Then he turned and faced the entire group of weapons buyers. "Hey, I know it's a pain in the ass for you guys, but think about it: you really want to be the only one without my kind of firepower when the rest have it?"

All the buyers glanced at each other.

"Before you answer that, let me give you that little demo I promised."

He reached into his pocket and brought out a remote-control switch. With a flick he started a large door on the back side of the big room.

Behind the door was the armored Hummer. Standing

beside the Hummer were Slats and four members of his gang, grinning and looking very cocky.

John Henry had no doubt that look was going to vanish very shortly. If Burke had killed his own partner, he surely wasn't going to let a bunch of street kids live.

"You remember the bankmobile?" Burke asked the buyers. "And the Boyz 'n the Hood? Who've served their purpose, incidentally."

Just as John Henry had feared, the gang's smiles faded like water down a drain. The overmuscled guard brought up his weapon and aimed it at the gang. Two of the other guards did the same, covering the kids in a cross fire.

"What's up with this, man?" Slats asked.

Burke laughed. "I always use expendable rats for preliminary testing."

Slats was angry. He moved quickly, but not fast enough.

"No," John Henry yelled, but it was too late.

The muscled guard fired, hitting Slats with a glancing blow from the balled lightning.

It spun Slats around once and into the Hummer. He was still alive.

"He's only stunned," Burke said, laughing as the other members of the gang slowly put their hands in the air. Suddenly they didn't look like such powerful gang members, but just young kids in deep trouble.

Steel stared at them, then at Sparks who looked as shocked as he felt. Something had to be done.

And done quickly.

But what?

Burke turned back to his weapons buyers. "You've seen how powerful these weapons are."

He paused and then smiled. "But gentlemen, I've now

developed a new one five times more powerful. Wait until you—''

Suddenly John Henry saw his opening. He let out a huge laugh, filling the large room with the barking sound.

Burke turned and stared at him, his face full of anger, his scar twitching.

"Only five times?" Steel said. "What have you got, a water pistol?" And again Steel laughed loud and long.

"And you've done better?" Burke asked, his voice hard and grating.

"Of course," Steel said. "My hammer's got more power than what you describe."

"That's hard to believe," Burke said.

Steel laughed. "See for yourself," he said. "I'll let my hammer speak for itself. Just slide the switch on the right forward."

Burke picked up the hammer and did as Steel suggested. A trigger popped out.

"Just don't twist the red switch or she'll be too hot for you to handle."

Burke glanced up at Steel. "Really?" he said, looking down at the hammer in his hand. "Well, let's see."

Burke indicated that the guard beside Steel step away. "I was planning to use you for my demonstration anyway."

"I'm honored," Steel said, but Burke ignored him.

"Killing two birds with one stone," he said. "It will be a pleasure."

Steel turned to the group of weapons buyers. "If he kills me, you'll all lose out."

Two of them shook their heads in disgust. The rest didn't even move.

"I'm afraid," Burke said to Steel, "that we don't need your help anymore, except as a target."

He raised the hammer to his shoulder and aimed it at Steel. Then he paused. "The red switch, huh?"

He pushed the switch to red. "Irons, you know I just have to push the envelope."

Then Burke pulled the trigger and the hammer flew out of his hands, slamming hard against John Henry's armor.

Steel flicked off the electromagnet and twisted the hammer up into position.

"Yeah, I know you do, Burke."

"Kill him," Burke said.

"Maybe not," Sparks said.

With a flick of her wrist she hit a switch on her wheelchair. A bright red laser beam shot out of the hand grip, burning into the wall near one of the guards.

Then she hit a second switch and her wheelchair started to spin like a top, sweeping the laser beam toward the guards and weapons buyers.

Everyone dove for cover, and instantly the room was pandemonium, pure and simple.

CHAPTER 42

THE NIGHT ROARED WITH THE RUMBLING SOUNDS OF two helicopters lifting off the Los Angeles Police Department's heli-pad. Around them the night lights of the city sparkled on the clear summer evening, filling the sky with light. The wind from the takeoff scattered paper and dust in hot, swirling clouds, forcing two cops below to cover their faces.

Colonel David sat in the copilot seat of the lead chopper.

"We're airborne," he said into a microphone. "We'll be there in less than five minutes."

"I hope you make it in time," the man over the satellite link said. "The place sounds like World War Three inside there."

"Understand," Colonel David said. "Just hang on."

He clicked off the call, then clicked another switch. "Did you get a trace on that?"

A moment later a voice came back over his headset. "No, sir."

"Damn," Colonel David said, staring out at the miles of lights stretched out in front of him.

He turned to the pilot. "Make this as fast as you can. I've got a bad feeling about this."

Slats and his gang ducked for cover behind the Hummer and nearby roof support pillars. Pistols appeared in their hands as if all of the gang had practiced quick-draw routines.

Steel ducked behind a column as Sparks' laser swept past him, leaving a burning path around the room.

She was gaining speed, cutting the laser off and on as she went around and around. But sitting there spinning like that, she was a very easy target.

Across the large room, one of Burke's professional guards was on his stomach on the concrete, pulling up his rifle and aiming it at Sparks.

Steel yanked the hammer to his shoulder and fired in one move. The ball of lightning smacked the guard in the side, flipping him over and over across the concrete. The guy smashed into a support pillar and didn't move.

Slats' gang opened up on the guards, suddenly joining Steel and Sparks's side of the battle. The bullets from their pistols bounced off the concrete, smacking into wood with sickening thumps. Their gunfire echoed around the big room like strings of firecrackers going off at once.

The arms buyers were scrambling for the door, alternately running and crawling to stay below Sparks' laser fire. They all looked like a herd of monkeys in black suits running in front of a charging lion.

Two of Burke's guards ducked from behind support columns and fired at Slats and his gang, forcing them to duck behind any cover they could find. Two of the fireballs missed their targets and ignited trash behind Slats.

Steel stepped forward to take another shot at the guards attacking the kids.

Suddenly Burke stepped out from behind a pillar, facing Steel. Burke sneered at Steel, his dark eyes intense, his face covered with sweat. He raised his rifle and in one motion fired.

Burke hadn't been too bad a shot in the service, and that thought instantly went through John Henry's mind as he reacted, ducking and rolling sideways.

The ball lightning missed him and smashed through a boarded-up window behind him.

Outside, the lightning ball smashed into an old tanker truck sitting next to the building. The truck exploded with a deafening roar, sending burning fuel and parts flying in every direction, including back through the window. There were now fires going in three different areas of the old mill.

Steel knew the place was going to be an inferno very, very quickly.

"Cover the Steel man," Slats shouted, and two of his gang laid down fire at Burke, bouncing bullets off the concrete floor at his feet.

Burke did a quick dive and rolled away to cover behind a pile of old crates.

Steel went the other way, ducking and running until he was next to Sparks.

She saw him coming and stopped the spinning on her chair, laying down laser cover at the guards.

In one movement he had her and the chair out of the open and behind the limited protection of a large column.

"Improvement on your chair, huh?" he said as he spun her around to face the battle.

"Hey," she said, breathless. "Give a girl a little free time, a couple of lasers, and—"

A burst of ball lightning chewed up the wall beside

them, sending an explosion of burning wood and hot metal showering in all directions.

Sparks adjusted her chair slightly, then snapped a switch on the underside of the armrest.

A sonic blast shot across the room in the direction of one of Burke's guards, blowing him sideways and right through the wooden wall of the building. The guard wouldn't be rejoining the battle any time soon.

"Why should you have all the fun?" she said, glancing up at Steel and smiling.

He just shook his head and pointed at one of the fires crackling up the old wood wall. "We gotta get you out of here quick."

"How's this for quick enough?" she said. "See you outside." With that, she hit another hidden switch on her chair. There was a loud whoosh of compressed air from the back of her chair and she was rocketing toward the open door.

The muscled guard tried to step out and take a shot at her as she went past.

"Oh, no you don't," Steel said. He raised his hammer and sent a burst of ball lightning into the pillar the guy had been hiding behind, spraying him with burning wood. The impact of the shot sent him spinning for cover.

A moment later Sparks was in the parking lot and moving away from the building at top speed. Steel just hoped she'd figured out some brakes for that chair, too— at least before she plowed into the fence between the mill and the steel factory.

"Payback's a bitch, huh, Burke?" Slats yelled while spraying Burke's hiding area with bullets.

But Steel could have warned Slats to never taunt Burke unless he was willing to pay the consequences. Timing the shots Slats had been firing, Burke stepped into the open and fired at the leader of the gang.

The fireball picked up the gang leader and knocked him backward. The impact flipped the kid over like a diver doing a back flip and smashed him into the huge electrical panel on the wall.

With the electrical charge of the shot and the impact of Slats against the panel, it short-circuited. The explosion sounded like a cannon going off inside the huge room.

An arching spark exploded off Slats, along with a huge cloud of ugly gray smoke.

Then every light flickered and went out, dropping the room into darkness, lit only by the orange light of the growing fires.

Steel watched as Slats stayed frozen against the electrical panel for a long second, then dropped face-first to the concrete. There was no doubt he was dead.

The rest of Slats' gang were pinned down and mostly out of ammunition. Two of Burke's guards were working their way toward the kids, who cowered behind support pillars.

Steel ducked around behind the Hummer, then behind the gang members. With a quick flick of his hammer, he set it for sonic burst and fired at the wall behind them.

The wall exploded outward like a truck had hit it at sixty miles per hour.

''Get out!'' Steel shouted to the boys, pointing at the hole he'd just created. ''Run! I'll cover you.''

He turned and faced the two guards, flicking his hammer back to full force.

He shot a ball of lightning at each. He caught one squarely in the chest, sending him over backward. The one with huge muscles was knocked down, but managed to scramble back to his feet and to cover.

Behind him the gang members scrambled outside and into the night.

Suddenly Burke stepped into the light of the fire and stopped near a door.

Steel raised his hammer and pointed it at Burke. "I suggest you give it up."

Burke only laughed, not even raising a gun. "First," he said, "let's see what's behind door number two."

With a quick flick he opened the door to what appeared to be an equipment closet.

Inside Martin stood, his hands tied, his mouth gagged. And his eyes completely filled with fear.

CHAPTER 43

UNCLE JOE HELD THE SONIC RIFLE IN HIS HAND AND moved across the mill yard, staying in the shadows.

In front of him the main building of the mill was on fire in half a dozen spots, and the flames were spreading across the roof. Anyone inside that building couldn't stay there much longer. At least not stay there and live.

The limos were all heading at top speed out the gate like it was a race. Uncle Joe supposed it was. But it was real good they were all gone. Less to worry about.

And less people involved.

From inside the big mill building, Uncle Joe could hear gunfire, then suddenly there was a large explosion and the lights went out.

"Uh-oh," he said, ducking and heading for a window on the ground floor, running as fast as his old legs would carry him.

Burke moved over and stood next to Martin, the sonic rifle barrel never pointing away from Martin's chest.

Steel kept the hammer aimed at Burke in the same way as around them the building continued to catch fire, the smoke slowly filling the big room with a choking orange-colored cloud.

"My new best friend," Burke said, indicating Martin and smiling. "Comfortable enough to come here on a field trip with ol' Mr. Large."

Steel said nothing.

Burke laughed, then got very serious. "Don't you understand, Johnny?" Burke said. "Success has never been enough for me. I always need to see my enemies *fall*."

Burke grabbed hold of Martin and held the kid in front of him, the rifle pointed at Martin's head.

Martin's eyes filled with panic, but the kid was smart enough to stay still.

Steel knew that at that range, Martin would be dead instantly if Burke pulled the trigger.

"Now," Burke said. "Why don't you move so Martin and I can take a drive."

He yanked Martin toward the Hummer just beyond where Steel stood.

"Guess again," a loud voice said from off to the right of Burke.

Uncle Joe was leaning in a broken window, the sonic cannon aimed straight at Burke's back.

But Burke was quicker.

He spun and fired.

The ball of fire smacked into the window frame and Uncle Joe, tossing him backward and out of Steel's sight.

John Henry's mind screamed, "No!"

Uncle Joe couldn't be hurt.

Then the fear of the thought turned to instant anger.

Burke would pay. And he would pay dearly for what he did to Sparks in Arizona.

And now to Uncle Joe.

As Burke spun and fired at Uncle Joe, Martin yanked free of his grip and ran at full speed toward a side door just behind and to the left of Steel.

Burke twisted around and again fired, this time right at Martin's back.

But this time Steel was faster.

He took two long running steps and dove, tackling Martin just as the shot went over both their heads and smashed into the wall, adding more flames to the already growing smoke and heat-filled room.

The momentum of Steel's tackle slid him and Martin through the open door and into a large room totally in flames. Every wall was engulfed.

Then, just as Steel pulled Martin to his feet, a grenade rolled into the room, the door slammed closed, and the clear sound of a bolt being slid shut echoed over the crackling of the flames.

"There's no way out!" Martin shouted.

Steel ducked down and scooped up the grenade. Using both hands, he held it against his armor. But there was no way his armor was going to be strong enough to completely stop a grenade at close range. And even if he covered it, Martin might get hurt.

He glanced quickly around. The only opening in the burning room was a round hole in the wall about fifteen feet up, right below the level of the smoke. It looked as if it had held a fan at one time in the distant past.

"There," Martin said, pointing at the hole. "Throw it. Quick!"

"Get down," Steel shouted to Martin.

Then with two quick steps he jumped, trying to get as far into the air as he could to be closer to the hole.

Then as if he'd been playing basketball his entire life, he lobbed the grenade through the hole.

Perfect shot.

Steel instantly turned and covered Martin with his armor as on the other side of the wooden wall the grenade exploded, blowing the door and a huge chunk of the wall into splinters.

"Let's go," Steel said, standing and yanking Martin to his feet. With a hard grasp on Martin's arm, they sprinted through the new opening back into the middle of the big room.

But now Burke was in the Hummer.

He leaned out the driver's window and shouted. "Hey, Johnny, you never got a chance to see my new toy, did you?"

The roof of the Hummer snapped back and a huge cannonlike weapon snapped up into place.

Burke smiled, the red scar dancing on his face like a snake. He climbed up behind the new weapon and stood there like a top gunner on a tank.

"Let's see how that armor of yours stands up to this."

John Henry had no idea what this new weapon was, but he instantly knew he was going to find out.

He grabbed Martin, pulled the kid against his chest, then turned his back on Burke and crouched, trying his best to use the thick area of his shield on his back to protect them.

The new weapon fired, smashing Steel and Martin into a nearby support pillar. But somehow Steel managed to stay in position, braced against the shot.

The heat on his back felt as if a branding iron were punching through his armor. To do that, the electrical power of that weapon must have been enormous.

Then a high-pitched human scream echoed through the room and the force and burning stopped.

Steel spun around.

Burke was airborne backward. Obviously his new weapon had backfired on him.

Or Steel's armor had reflected the beam backward.

Something Burke hadn't counted on had happened, that was for sure.

Burke smashed into a supporting beam twenty feet behind the Hummer. The burning ceiling above him crashed down, covering Burke in flames.

There was one more scream from him, then nothing.

Steel took a deep breath and glanced around. He and Martin were the last people inside the building.

Everything around them was on fire.

"How are we going to get out?" Martin shouted over the roaring sound of the flames.

Steel had no answer for him.

He wasn't sure there was an answer.

CHAPTER 44

TO SPARKS, SITTING IN HER WHEELCHAIR IN THE parking lot, the mill building looked like an inferno. She could feel the heat from the flames shooting from the roof, and most of the nearby wall was totally engulfed in fire.

And John Henry was still inside.

The armor wouldn't protect him from this kind of heat. It would cook his flesh instead. He had to get out of there, and soon.

Suddenly an explosion near one side of the building caught her attention.

A man flopped backward away from the wall, landing on his back on the concrete.

For a moment her mind didn't register what she was seeing, then it dawned on her that the man who had just exploded away from the side of the building was Uncle Joe.

With a quick twist of one wheel, she started toward that edge of the burning building, hitting her air boost to rocket her chair across the now-empty parking lot.

It seemed to take forever to reach him. And the closer she got, the more the intensity of the heat beat at her face and arms. It felt as if any moment her hair would just catch fire.

She skidded the chair to a stop right over the body. Above him the window had been blown out, and flames shot from the opening like a blowtorch.

"Uncle Joe!" she shouted over the roaring noise of the fire. "Uncle Joe!"

He stirred and blinked, but didn't move to get up.

"Help me," she shouted to him. "We've got to get away from here. Now!"

With her left hand firmly grasping the wheelchair handle, she reached down with her right hand and grabbed Uncle Joe by the arm, pulling him up toward her.

He managed to help a little, but not much.

Somehow, she managed to get him up and across her lap, his feet dangling over one handle and his head over the other.

She spun the wheelchair around, then yanked Uncle Joe up solidly on her stomach. "Keep your hands away from the wheels and hold on!" she shouted as behind her the walls of the mill seemed to explode.

She hit both the air jets and a special rocket-style jet she'd mounted low off the center of her chair.

For a moment she wasn't sure if the jets were going to knock her over, but then, almost as if the chair had a balance of its own, it shoved her forward, away from the burning building.

Behind her a wall of the mill was collapsing in on itself, covering the area where she and Uncle Joe had been the moment before.

It felt as if John Henry's skin was cooking inside the armor. He'd planned for the metal to take bullets, and sonic charges, and shotgun blasts. But he'd never planned on being inside a thin steel shell in a hot fire. There was no way he was going to last much longer.

"This way," Steel shouted to Martin over the roar of the fire as sparks rained down on them from all sides.

He grabbed Martin by the arm and yanked him toward the Hummer. He snapped open the driver's door and tossed Martin in across the seat, then climbed in behind the wheel. His head banged against the ceiling and his knees were jammed against the dashboard, but somehow he fit.

The huge room was now almost gone, buried under a thick cloud of smoke and burning lumber. Being trapped inside the armored Hummer was going to be as bad as being out in the open in the fire.

Maybe worse. The death would be slower.

Steel shouted to Martin. "Seat belt! Hang on!"

He twisted the key and felt the Hummer kick to life.

"Let's see how strong this beast really is."

He spun the Hummer's wheel and hit the gas at the same time. The Hummer slid sideways for a moment, then the tires caught traction and accelerated directly for the burning wall of the mill.

"Oh, shit!" Martin screamed.

Steel just gripped the wheel tight and kept his foot hard on the accelerator.

The Hummer smashed into the burning wall and went right on through.

In the cab it felt like the entire car had been rammed. Steel's head snapped forward, but his armor protected him when he hit the steering wheel with his forehead.

Martin had done as Steel had ordered and buckled up, but he got bounced around real good.

The Hummer went sideways off the slight drop outside the wall.

Steel managed to correct the slide just enough to keep them from flipping over, then he gunned the Hummer away from the burning building.

Ahead of him Sparks was flashing along in her wheelchair, Uncle Joe over her lap.

Steel felt a huge wave of relief flood over him, and all he could do was laugh.

Sparks couldn't believe her bad luck. She'd managed to get Uncle Joe on her chair and away from the fire, but now Burke's Hummer was headed directly for the fence and the gate back to Uncle Joe's van, on a direct course to cut her off.

She snapped off the air jets and slowed the chair quickly, looking around for any way to escape. On her lap Uncle Joe was moaning and starting to move. She didn't have much time.

In front of her the Hummer slid to a stop, both doors popped open, and Martin climbed out the side closest to her.

Martin!

What was he doing here?

And in Burke's machine?

Then Steel got out the driver's-side door and came around the front of the Hummer.

"All right!" she shouted as Steel ran toward her.

Her heart pounded, seemingly right up into her throat. Until that moment she hadn't really realized just how deep her feelings for John Henry Irons were. But almost losing him made them very, very clear.

She braked to a stop and looked up into the eyes of John Henry as he bent over her. She could tell he was hurting in a number of places, and his bright steel armor was black with soot. But he was the best-looking thing she had ever seen.

"Really glad to see you," she said softly.

"And you," he said. He bent down and looked at Uncle Joe's face.

"This here is a young'un's sport," Uncle Joe said, trying to push himself up, but failing.

John Henry glanced up at Sparks and laughed. "I think he's going to be all right. I'll take him to the van."

"Colonel on the way," Uncle Joe said loud enough for Sparks to hear.

"We need to get out of here now," she said, glancing up at Steel. "Unless we want to have a very long conversation with Colonel David."

Steel lifted Uncle Joe off her lap and cradled him in his arms like he was a child. She could feel Uncle Joe's weight gone from her lap. And with it a sense of relief flooded over her.

They all headed for the gate into the steel yard and Uncle Joe's van.

John Henry couldn't believe how much relief he felt. And how numb. They had managed to accomplish what they had started. The weapons were off the streets, and Burke was gone.

Just inside the steel-yard gate, Uncle Joe glanced up at John Henry and said, "Better tell someone there's one of Burke's men tied up back there in them piles of steel."

John Henry laughed. "We'll tell them."

As they reached Uncle Joe's junk van, Martin held the back door open for Steel to put Uncle Joe inside.

"You're Johnny, aren't you?" Martin said.

"Get in the van," Steel said.

"Choppers coming," Sparks said, pointing to the east.

"This is dope," Martin said. "My own brother is Steel. I want to help."

Steel picked up Sparks and sat her gently in the passenger seat, then slid her wheelchair in beside Uncle Joe in the back.

"I could be like Robin," Martin said. "I could get a cape and—"

"Martin," Steel said, staring at the kid. "You want to know what you can do?"

"What?" Martin shouted. "Anything."

"Don't say anything to Grandma," Steel said. "Now. Get. In. The. Van."

Martin did as he was told, and before the choppers were over the burning mill Steel had the van headed down a side street, carefully staying at the speed limit as if he drove this path every day.

Beside him Sparks sat smiling.

And under his armor, Steel knew he was smiling, too.

CHAPTER 45

THE BASKETBALL COURT AT THE CORNER PARK ONLY held three teenagers on this hot afternoon. And they were only shooting, not really playing, waiting for a fourth so they could have a game. All three wore only shorts and no gang colors.

The bigger of the kids was named Holdecker. He had been Slats' number two man in the Marks. He'd been one of the gang members lucky enough to get out of the burning mill the night Slats was killed.

"I heard he broke them fools off something ugly," the shorter of the three boys said, talking about Steel.

The other short kid took a quick shot. "He's like this giant ten-foot superrobot. He kicks everybody's ass."

"He ain't no robot," Holdecker said. "He's a man, but he's more than that."

"Whatever," one of the others said. "He needs to be sporting colors."

Holdecker stopped, holding the ball and staring at the other kid. "Don't be talking that gang shit no more."

"What's up with you, homey? Ain't you a Mark?"

"Not no more," Holdecker said. "Ain't no more Marks. That gang shit's played out, man. Wake up."

Holdecker flipped the ball at the kid and walked away. Both the younger boys watched him go, amazed.

And very much impressed.

Colonel David's office was what a civilian might expect of a military office. Two metal desks, a number of pictures and citations on the plain white walls. A window looking out over the green lawn and the base beyond.

"I'm glad you called," Colonel David said into the phone while motioning for a young woman lieutenant at the other desk to work quickly on the trace from the other phone line. "The guard we found tied up in the steel yard talked his head off. Fingered Burke all the way down the line."

The colonel nodded at something said on the phone. "Not yet," he said. "We're still raking the rubble for his teeth. And the guard showed us another tape on the bank job that showed one of the gang kids firing at the chopper. That means you're completely cleared."

Colonel David glanced at the lieutenant with a "hurry it up" look.

"Not yet," the lieutenant whispered. "Keep them talking."

The colonel shook his head in disgust and sat down.

In the junk dome John Henry, Sparks, and Uncle Joe all listened in to the conversation with Colonel David. Sparks had rigged up a special computer program that made John Henry's voice sound exactly like Arnold Schwarzenegger's. *Exactly.*

"Who are you behind that mask?" the colonel asked.

"Doesn't really matter, does it?" John Henry said.

"I've accomplished all I wanted to. You won't see me anymore."

"What?" Colonel David yelled into the phone.

Both Sparks and Uncle Joe almost broke out laughing.

"Now hang on," Colonel David went on, almost sputtering. "We might be able to do some good work together in the future. I'd even consider giving you access to that hot Hummer we got from Burke. You could—"

"Colonel," John Henry said, calmly breaking into the colonel's speech. "Tracing this call is a waste of time. Your com data person's gonna think we're in—"

John Henry glanced at Sparks.

"Cincinnati," she whispered.

"Cincinnati," John Henry said.

Back in Colonel David's office the lieutenant jumped to her feet. "Got them," she said.

Colonel David looked over at her.

"They're in a diner in Cincinnati," she said. "Should I—"

"Forget it, Lieutenant," Colonel David said. "That will be all for now."

He waited until she was out of the room, then focused on the phone.

"Listen, Ahh-nold," he said. "I know this isn't your real voice. Just tell me the truth, goddamnit. Is this you, *Irons*?"

"Can't talk anymore, Colonel," John Henry said. "Phone might not be secure. I'll be in touch."

The phone at the colonel's ear went dead.

"Damn you, Irons," the colonel said, replacing the phone. But as he did so he was smiling.

*   *   *

The intensive care unit of a hospital burn ward was the most sterile place in a hospital. And it always reeked of the smell of burning flesh. Many nurses and some doctors couldn't work this ward because of that smell.

At the moment the ward only had one patient, a man who had given his name as Bill Whitaker.

A doctor stood beside the nurse at the end of the man's bed, reading his chart.

"What's his story?" the doctor asked, flipping the chart closed and shaking his head.

"Hikers found him along an arroyo near the river. He said his sleeping bag had caught fire. No family."

"Probably just as well," the doctor said. "With all those burns, nobody would recognize him anyhow. It's amazing he's still alive."

In the background of the ward a radio news report came on. The announcer said, "It's been confirmed that the mysterious armored man known only as Steel was primarily responsible for exposing, and foiling, a huge international plan to sell high-tech weapons."

The burned man on the bed moaned, then in a whisper that didn't make it past his bandages, he said, "It . . . isn't . . . over . . . Irons."

CHAPTER 46

SIX MONTHS AFTER THE BIG MILL FIRE, GRANDMA Odessa opened Grandma Odessa's Black and Bleu Restaurant just four blocks from her home. The place had a natural, down-home feel, with fancy tablecloths and the most expensive silverware John Henry could find.

Tonight, the day before the official opening, the place was packed with only friends from the neighborhood, there to help her and her staff test the food. And work out some of the bugs before opening the doors to paying customers.

Grandma Odessa hurried out of the kitchen and greeted John Henry, Sparks, Martin, and Uncle Joe as they came through the front door.

John Henry leaned down and kissed her forehead. "The place smells and looks wonderful."

"Thank you," she said, squeezing his hand and smiling up at him. Then she pointed to a corner table. "A special family table," she said.

They all moved into their positions. John Henry sat

on the outside so his legs could stretch out. And so that he could sit next to Sparks. Since the night at the mill they hadn't been far apart for long.

"Who is this Al Fresco guy, anyway?" Uncle Joe asked.

Grandma Odessa frowned at him, then pointed to a chair. "Just sit down there, Joe. Use that mouth for something other than wisecracking."

"I'll have today's special, please," Martin said, enunciating each syllable. He'd been spending the last two months learning how to speak more formally. He claimed it was much harder than street talk.

"Maybe you should find out what it is, first," John Henry said.

Grandma Odessa smiled. "Lobster served out of the shell with a sweet-potato cream sauce garnished with crisped okra."

Sparks laughed. "Grandma Odessa, you *are* amazing."

"No, you want to see amazing," she said. She turned and hurried into the kitchen, then a moment later was back carrying the most beautifully brown soufflé.

"You did it," John Henry said. "You actually made a hominy soufflé."

"Of course I did," Grandma Odessa said, smiling. "Ain't it something? What a person can do when they put their mind to it." She glanced at John Henry with a knowing look.

He knew exactly what she meant. She was very proud of what he had done as Steel, even though she didn't "officially" know. But there was very little that got past her.

"Yes, ma'am," John Henry said. "It sure is. When you get the right kind of help." He smiled at Sparks and she smiled back.

"Oh," Sparks said, "since Grandma Odessa's showing off her creation, maybe we should show them my new one."

"Now?" John Henry asked, smiling.

"Now," Sparks said.

She swung her wheelchair slightly away from the table so that it faced John Henry. Then with a flick of a switch, a small motor somewhere on her chair started a faint whirring sound.

Slowly the chair straightened upward, lifting and holding her in a standing position.

John Henry laughed and stood facing her as the chair lifted her up and up until she stood tall enough to be face-to-face with John Henry.

"I love it," John Henry said, putting his arms around her and giving her a huge hug and kiss.

"So do I," Sparks said, kissing him back.

At the table, and around the restaurant, everyone applauded and cheered.

So they kissed again.